HIRED GIRLFRIEND, PREGNANT FIANCÉE?

HIRED GIRLFRIEND, PREGNANT FIANCÉE?

NINA MILNE

MILLS & BOON

First published in Great Britain 2019
by Mills & Boon, an imprint of HarperCollins*Publishers*
1 London Bridge Street, London, SE1 9GF

Large Print edition 2019

© 2019 Nina Milne

ISBN: 978-0-263-08269-2

MIX
Paper from
responsible sources
FSC **FSC® C007454**

This book is produced from independently certified
FSC™ paper to ensure responsible forest management. For
more information visit www.harpercollins.co.uk/green.

Printed and bound in Great Britain
by CPI Group (UK) Ltd, Croydon, CR0 4YY

To Clara—for being a fabulous friend *and* for reading all of my books in a very short space of time!

CHAPTER ONE

WHAT ON EARTH was she doing here? Gabby Johnson forced a smile to her face and her nerves into submission as the word *mistake* flashed through her mind in neon. *Get a grip, Gabby.* This was supposed to be fun, for heaven's sake— a hen weekend, friends together for two days of female solidarity and a good time to be had by all.

The problem was it depended on your definition of a good time.

'Right!' The maid of honour, to whom Gabby had just been introduced, a vivacious petite redhead called Lorna, clapped her hands together. 'Ladies, I have a timetable of fun activities planned to celebrate the upcoming wedding of our very lovely friend Charlotte.'

Gabby relaxed slightly as everyone cheered. She reminded herself that this *was* a celebration—that it had been *kind* of Charlotte to include Gabby. They had been friends in college, lost touch and then reignited a friendship of sorts after bumping into each other a few months ago.

'OK,' Lorna continued. 'So here we are in the lovely city of Bath, in this fantastic house right in the centre, and this is our plan for the evening. I promise that cocktails will be involved later. But first, I have a fun activity planned. Before I explain that, it's time to have a glass of bubbly whilst we all get changed.' Lorna turned around and gestured to seven luminous pink bags. 'These are all named, and I hope I have got the sizes roughly right.'

Gabby stepped forward with everyone else and took her designated bag, watching as everyone else peered into theirs, listening to their shrieks of laughter. Panic began to shrivel the edges of her introverted soul.

Come on, Gabby. Woman up. How bad can it be?

The pops of champagne corks as everyone pulled mini bottles from their bags should have reassured her, but then…

'It's a bunny suit!' one of the women exclaimed. 'I have always wanted to try one of these on.'

A bunny suit? Somehow she'd expected a more low-key affair. Dinner and drinks. Maybe a cocktail. Bunny suits hadn't figured anywhere in the equation. Now she was going to spend the evening in one.

Why, oh, why couldn't she be like all the other women in the room, who seemed enthused by the whole idea? She would have sold her rapidly contracting soul in exchange for some of the palpable joie de vivre and confidence that filled the room.

Gazing into the contents of the bag, she forced herself to maintain a smile as she tugged the costume out. A bright pink corset, a pom-pom tail, bunny ears, sheer tights… Now she understood why she'd been asked to bring a pair of pink stilettos.

Ideas streamed through her mind: perhaps she could fake illness, perhaps she could object on the grounds of political correctness…? *Get a grip, Gabby.* There was nothing worse than a party pooper, so all she could do was exchange her jeans and T-shirt for the bunny outfit.

Somehow she had to loosen up. Her childhood mantra ran through her head—*in twenty-four hours it will be over.* It came from the times when she'd been scared, hiding in whatever sanctuary she'd been able to find whilst her mother partied.

Even aged three she'd known with chilling certainty that her mother would not be able to keep her safe, would be too far under the influence of drugs and alcohol. So she had always scoped out a place to conceal herself—in a cupboard, under a bed… And wherever she'd been she'd kept telling herself that she would get through it, that at this time tomorrow it would be over. Comparatively speaking, parading the streets in a bunny suit would be a doddle.

'You OK?' Charlotte had moved next to her in her bridal bunny costume. 'I know this probably isn't your cup of tea, but…'

'Don't be silly. It's a laugh,' Gabby managed and adjusted her bunny ears with an enthusiasm she hoped came across as genuine.

Time to douse her inner cringe. Irritation threshed at her nerves—*why* couldn't she take this in the right spirit and have fun? It wouldn't be that bad; she was in a group of eight, all dressed the same—she could just fade into the background. After all, that was one of her best skills.

'OK, ladies. Gather round!' Lorna called as

she produced her next exhibit—a pink top hat. 'This hat contains eight challenges. Each of us will take one and then off we'll go to attempt the challenges. We'll pretty much stick together, but I do require photographic proof that the challenges have been completed!'

Fabulous. Even her fade-into-the-background skills would struggle to provide invisibility in this situation. And what sort of challenge?

Panic began to twist in her tummy. Gabby might chafe against her introvert nature, but she accepted it as a cast-iron personality trait. Acknowledged that it had helped keep her invisible and under the radar when she'd most needed to, and had kept her safe amidst the chaos of her mother's lifestyle. Then later, after the horror of her mum's death—the result of an overdose—Gabby's quietness, her 'invisibility', had meant she had been allowed to live with her grandparents despite her social worker's concerns about their ages.

'Read it! Read it! Read it!'

The chant pulled Gabby back to the here and now and she realised that someone had pulled the first challenge from the hat.

'"Exchange an item of clothing with a man you don't know."'

Gabby looked on as everyone laughed, and felt anxiety tornado as Lorna held the hat out to her.

Breathe. In twenty-four hours this will be over. Her dignity would be in tatters, but it would be over.

Inwardly praying, she pulled out a slip of paper and looked down at it. Someone, somewhere *had* to be kidding.

'Read it! Read it! Read it!'

Stomach hollow, she did just that. '"Find a hot stranger and get a kiss on camera."'

This caused much merriment and Gabby forced herself to join in, etching a smile on her face in a gallant attempt to join in the spirit of the occasion. Time to channel personality trait number two—the art of faking it. Throughout childhood she'd made sure she'd played a part— whatever part she'd needed to play to survive.

A couple of hours later, as afternoon segued into the beginning of evening, her cheek muscles ached and her panic had escalated to the point of a need for a paper bag to breathe into. All around her Kate, Charlotte, Lorna, et al. had danced and spun through their challenges, and soon it would be only Gabby left. She would be the focus of attention.

Moisture sheened her neck, even as she maintained the smile and her brain raced.

At that moment Lorna moved over to her, a friendly smile on her face. 'Gabby, it's just you now. How can we help? Or if you want to give it a miss, it's no big deal. I should have known that this wouldn't be everyone's thing. If you want to skip it, then it's not a problem. We can head straight to the cocktail place.'

For a moment Gabby nearly collapsed in relief at the opt-out clause—but then sheer annoyance at herself surfaced. Did she want to be the one person on this hen do who didn't complete her challenge? The one person who didn't provide a photograph for the album Lorna would be putting together for Charlotte to look back on? Dammit—she *had* to try.

Keeping her lips upturned and her body relaxed, she even managed a laugh that hopefully held insouciance.

'Actually, would it be OK if I slip off by myself and give it a go? I could meet you at the cocktail place after.'

'Sure. That works.'

So, challenge in her hand, tugging at the ridiculous bunny suit, Gabby Johnson ventured forth into the dusk.

Zander Grosvenor looked around the table and reminded himself that he was an ultrasuccessful multimillionaire, not a scrubby schoolboy any more. Yet, as he surveyed the faces of his mother and two elder sisters, it was hard to hold on to that fact.

His father had clearly had the right idea when he'd absconded to the golf course This felt way too reminiscent of those awful sit-down chats from when he *had* been a schoolboy—and a very unsuccessful one at that. For a moment the remembered burn of frustrated humiliation, the sting of failure, pinged his nerves. He remembered the knowledge of his own stupidity, the knowledge that he couldn't live up to the bar set by his sisters however hard he tried. Hell, he couldn't even manage to read a baby book.

Enough. That was the past. And it had been resolved when eventually he had been diagnosed with dyslexia. So simple an explanation, and yet it had occurred to no one. And that was why they were sitting here now—the Grosvenor family.

His mother had been racked with guilt that she hadn't realised sooner and, once the diagnosis had been made, had supported him every step of the way—as had his father. Julia, his eldest sister—ten years his senior—was now a successful human rights lawyer, divorced with two children, one of whom had just been diagnosed with dyslexia, too. Gemma was a successful surgeon, four years older than Zander, and engaged to Alessio Bravanti, internationally successful racing driver and Zander's best friend.

The four of them had gathered here to discuss the fundraiser he had organised and would host to raise money for and awareness of dyslexia. For a minute the reminder of his duties as host, the need to make a speech, twanged his nerves with anxiety. *Not now, Zander.* He'd manage it; he'd tamed his fear of public speaking and it wouldn't get the better of him at such an important event.

It was an event his family all wanted to be a part of, and he was grateful for that. Yet as he looked around the table he had the distinct impression of a hidden agenda.

'OK, everyone. It's a week until the event, so I thought we should go through any last-minute details.'

'Good idea,' his mother said breezily. 'I've invited Brenda Davison to the gala. She's just back from two years in Oz. She had an incredible time there and she is *such* a well-rounded person. Really interesting. I think you'd like her, Zan.'

Gemma beamed at him. 'And of course you remember Louise Martin. I asked her to attend the gala, but she's busy that day so I've asked her to the wedding instead. She's exactly your type.'

Zander blinked. 'That wasn't the sort of last-minute detail I had in mind,' he said sharply. Aware that he might have raised his voice a touch more than necessary, he tried a smile. 'I'd like to look down the auction list, talk about the caterers—not listen to a staged intervention on my love life.'

'It's not an "intervention on your love life" because you don't *have* one,' Julia pointed out gently. 'We're not trying to interfere. We want to help.'

'I don't need help.' Reminding himself that his family had the best intentions, that he loved them dearly and that love was mutual, Zander tried to keep his voice even.

His mother let out a small sigh and he could see the worry in her grey eyes. 'Sweetheart, Claudia wouldn't have wanted you to never have another relationship. It's been five years now since she died.'

'I know that.' Aware of the tautness of his tone, he tried to soften it. 'I am fine, Mum. Truly.'

Laura Grosvenor shook her head. 'We're not suggesting you remarry or enter into a long-term relationship...'

'Our suggestion is just to go out there and date... Have some fun,' Gemma said.

'When I want to do that, I will.'

Julia leant forward, blonde hair swinging, and touched his arm. 'We just hate to see you still grieving so much. We know you loved Claudia, and none of us will ever forget her, but we all think it's time for you to move on.'

For a second he closed his eyes, couldn't meet his family's gaze as the guilt stabbed him.

Yes, he had loved Claudia; they had been childhood sweethearts and he had worshipped the ground she'd walked on. They had swept into marriage aged twenty, full of optimism and hope for the future. But it had turned out their visions of that future were polar opposites, and soon Zander had known that they had made a mistake—that *he* had made a mistake.

It was a knowledge he had never shared—not with Claudia, not with his family, not with anyone. Because he would never have reneged on the vows he had made. Because whilst *his* feelings had changed, Claudia's hadn't. And then illness and tragedy had struck.

And after Claudia's death what had he done? Zander Grosvenor, grieving widower, had decided to follow his vision of the future, pursued his own dream and achieved phenomenal success. Accomplished a life and found fulfilment he would never have experienced if his wife had lived.

Sensing the heaviness of the silence, he opened his eyes. 'Look. I appreciate your concerns. I really do. But truly I am happy with my love life as it is.' *As in non-existent.* 'So, please, no more worrying. And no more matchmaking, OK?'

'OK...'

Three heads nodded, two blonde and one dark, but Zander didn't believe a word of it. Pushing his chair back, he rose to his feet. 'I'll be back soon—I need to go to the shops. Anyone want anything?'

Minutes later, he strode towards Bath's town

centre, hoping the exercise would dispel the fumes of guilt, but knowing they wouldn't.

His family cared about him, but how he wished they would respect his decision to eschew the world of relationships. In their defence, they didn't understand the truth. Of course he grieved for Claudia—grieved the loss of life so young, the tragic waste, the loss of the girl he had once loved. But it was a tainted grief, besmirched by the cold, hard knowledge that if Claudia had lived, he wouldn't be the person he was today.

On impulse he turned towards the abbey, made his way through the throng of people and headed for a place of cool walls and sanctuary. A place to look at the architecture, think of history and seek assuagement of the emotional turmoil that thoughts of Claudia still evoked five years since her death.

As he approached the imposing grandeur of the sandstone spires, touched by the orange rays of the setting sun, a flash of pink distracted him. A woman stood irresolute in the courtyard—a woman clad in a pink bunny suit. Not the usual garb for a visit to the abbey.

In the shadow of the abbey walls he could see her serious expression, her enormous hazel eyes filled with doubt, a straight nose, generous mouth. Glossy chestnut hair topped by pink bunny ears fell in a sleek curtain to her shoulders.

As if deciding to abandon her plan for entry, she turned and recognition jolted his brain. He wasn't sure why—who *was* she?

Her gaze met his in a fleeting skim; he saw an answering recognition and then she ducked her head and made to step past him. Just as memory kicked in.

'Gabby?' She'd been in the year below him and Claudia at high school.

For a moment he thought she'd deny it, and then she gave a small reluctant nod. 'Yes. I'm surprised you remember me.'

The memory came back. A young Zander, seventeen years old, walking down the school corridor as a tall slim girl with glossy chestnut hair came towards him, a pile of books clutched to her chest. As she'd passed, the books had cascaded to the floor and he'd automatically bent down to pick them up. He'd recognised the title of one, more from familiarity than an ability to decipher the words, but at least he'd seen the film.

They'd engaged in a conversation. He'd played the cool kid, one who didn't bother with books because films were way better, and she'd been so earnest in her disagreement that he could still recall her expression. Then Claudia had suddenly appeared. He'd later found out she had been alerted by a 'well-wishing friend'. Within seconds the chestnut-haired girl had been graciously dismissed and Zander had been swept away.

His attempts at remonstrance had been met with a shake of the head.

Dropped her books by accident? Don't be stupid, Zan. That girl—Gabby Johnson—likes you. I know I've got nothing to worry about, but she's a bit of a dark horse. No one knows much about her except that she lives with her grandparents. I just wanted her to know you're taken.

In the here and now, he decided there was little point in reliving the details. 'I do,' he settled for saying. 'So, how have you been?'

'Fine. I'm sorry about Claudia.' The words were simple but sincere, and, to his relief, she left it at that. No intrusive questions or additional sympathy.

'Thank you.'

'Right, well. Nice to see you again. I'll leave you to go in.'

As she moved forward, a piece of paper fluttered from her hand and she looked down at it, made to reach for it and then clearly recalled that she was wearing a bunny suit.

'We must stop meeting like this.' Zander squatted down and rose. He handed her the paper, his gaze inadvertently taking in the words. *Challenge No. 8.* The penny dropped. 'Hen party?'

'No,' she said, deadpan. 'I usually parade around Bath dressed like this.'

'Lucky Bath.' OK. That was *not* what he had meant to say. But somewhere between his brain and his mouth, that was what had come out.

Gabby stared at him. 'No. *Not* lucky Bath— and definitely not lucky me. Would *you* like to parade the streets dressed like this? Or the male equivalent, whatever that is. How about in a pair of tighty-whities?'

There was a silence as they both contemplated the scenario. Her face turned pink and her look of appraisal morphed into one of confusion. 'And bunny ears,' she added.

'Probably not many women's fantasy.' *Another vocal miscue.* 'Not, of course, that a bunny suit features in *my* fantasies. At all.' *And that was worse.* It was obvious that it had been a long time since he'd interacted socially with a woman. Time for a subject change. 'Anyway—did you manage the challenge?'

'Nope. Not yet. I thought I'd come to the abbey and have a bit of time out...maybe come up with a strategy. Or even some courage would do. But I don't feel comfortable going in dressed like this. It doesn't seem right. Plus I'm nearly out of time, so I'd better get going.'

'Maybe I can help?'

This caused her to pause. 'Why would you want to help?'

'I'm a nice guy. I wouldn't like you to fail a challenge. Old times' sake. Take your pick. So, what is the challenge?'

Reluctance warred with the hope on her face.

'I need to get a photo of myself kissing a h—a...a stranger.'

Ah. This was what happened when you started a social interaction with a woman dressed in a bunny suit. Not that it was a problem; a simple peck on the cheek and they could both go their separate ways. Yet his awareness of her ratcheted up. His gaze skimmed the smattering of freckles on the bridge of her nose, the impossible density and length of her eyelashes, the glossy lushness of those kissable lips.

Stop. What was the matter with him? He quite simply didn't look at women like this—hadn't done since Claudia. The sooner he got this over with the better.

'OK. I'll help. I know we aren't technically strangers, but it's close enough.'

Uncertainty touched her features and then she expelled a sigh. 'OK. Let's get it over with.'

Despite the echo of his own sentiment, he felt irrational chagrin touch him.

As if she sensed his reaction, she reached out and touched his arm. 'Sorry. That came out wrong. This is just a highly embarrassing situation for me. I'm a university librarian. An introvert. Being dressed like this... Asking someone to kiss me for a selfie is... I feel like an idiot. That's what I meant. But what I *should* have said is thank you—I really appreciate this.'

'No worries—and it's not a big deal. Where shall we pose?'

They moved to the side of the entrance.

'Here is fine.' Reaching into her small clutch bag, she pulled out her phone. 'OK. I'm ready.'

Zander leant forward and aimed for her cheek, ridiculously aware of her elusive flower scent, the smoothness of her skin and the glint of the chestnut sheen of her hair. Then at the last second she moved slightly, presumably in an attempt to position the shot, and instead of her cheek, his lips brushed hers.

Of course the right thing to do—the sensible action, the gentlemanly option—would have been to draw back. But that didn't happen. Instead he froze, caught in a sudden surge of sensation, tantalised, yearning, preternaturally aware.

Gabby drew in the slightest of breaths, and that triggered something else. Did he pull her forward? Did she step towards him? He didn't know and it didn't matter. Because all he could think about was the imperative need to deepen the kiss.

Her lips were soft, pliant against his, and somehow—impossibly—it felt as though they were the only two beings bathed in the last rays of sunshine that hazed around them and added magic to the ambience. Strands of desire twined together into a knot of longing in his gut as Gabby gave a small moan, pressed against him, looped her hands round his waist.

Until the spell was broken as a teenager jostled them, then jumped back with an embarrassed muttered apology.

Gabby, too, moved backwards in a jerky movement, hazel eyes wide in shock, her breathing fast. 'I... I...'

But clearly speech had deserted her, and without another word she spun round and walked away, her pace rapid. For a moment he opened his mouth to call her back—and then closed it again.

Bad idea. Bad move. Since Claudia's death Zander had eschewed the whole dating scene for a reason. Too complex. Too confusing. Too *complicated.* Just like that kiss had been.

And so he stood still and watched Gabby walk away.

CHAPTER TWO

GABBY HAD NEVER been so glad to see Monday morning arrive, and as soon as she entered the university library the world felt a better place. The feeling was further enhanced by the fact that she was dressed in cropped navy trousers and a cream blouse, her hair caught up in a pony-tail, without so much as a vestige of pink, let alone any bunny motifs, in sight. Even better, she was surrounded by the familiar dense quiet of her workplace—a blanket of calm after the neon pink of the weekend.

Sure, she'd enjoyed herself, but it had been overwhelming, as well. The fact she didn't re-ally know the other women very well but they knew each other had been an eerie reminder of her early life. As a child she had always been the outsider looking in—too shy, too awkward, too scared to try to join in. Cliques and friendship groups had formed and she'd missed the boat.

But those days were behind her, and as she

walked towards her office, the library environ-
ment offered a comforting mix of technology
and history, computers mingled with shelves of
books—all enough to propel the weekend into
the dim and dark recess of her memory.

Well, most of it anyway.

It would take a while before that kiss ceased to
haunt her—days later she'd swear her lips still
tingled. Ironically, the only physical evidence
that the kiss had even happened—the sole picture she'd managed to take—had come out so
blurry as to be useless. On her way back to the
party she'd entered an upmarket fashion store,
located a mannequin and he'd been her 'hot
stranger'. If only she'd thought of that earlier.

However, even if she *had* snapped That Kiss,
and had the guts to display it, she'd have been
disqualified anyway—kissing your teenage hero
probably didn't count as a 'hot stranger'.

Back in high school she had liked Zander Grosvenor—but not because of his looks or his rebel-
lious cool kid image or even his prowess on the
sporting field. It had never occurred to her that
she could have a chance with him and that had
been fine with her. Admiration from afar had
suited her, because perversely she'd liked him

because of his evident loyalty to his girlfriend. True, Claudia had been one of the prettiest, most popular girls in school but nonetheless...he had never so much as glanced at anyone else.

And she'd admired that; the traits she still valued were loyalty and trust. So she hadn't acknowledged that her interest in him was a crush, even though his presence had always brought on her nerves and she'd had to fight the impulse to try to 'accidentally' be wherever he was. The one time she had genuinely bumped into him by mistake had been so nerve-racking she'd dropped her books and actually had a conversation with him.

Enough. That was the dim and distant past and now she needed to banish Zander Grosvenor from her mind—and her lips, for that matter. At twenty-nine she was way too old to crush on anyone, let alone a man like the one Zander had become. Rich, successful...not her type at all. Time to focus on work.

Her day was divided between a reclassification project, a stint on the front desk and work on an online course she was putting together to help students access relevant information—more than enough to absorb her attention. So, apart from the occasional memory lapse to Planet Kiss, she was on her way back to 'Gabby as normal'. Enough so that at the end of the day she was able to close down her computer and look forward to a quiet evening at home.

The actual library was still open, and as she walked through the book-lined area she exchanged pleasantries with a few of the students. She stopped at one of the tables to pick up a couple of books that had been left, turned—and her sandal-clad feet screeched to a halt. Surely it couldn't be...? *Zander Grosvenor?* Her imagination must be messing with her head.

But then, there he was.

'Hi, Gabby.'

'Zander,' she said, and her voice echoed as hollow as her tummy.

For an insane second Gabby considered a dive beneath the table—though what she hoped *that* would achieve she had no idea. She needed to remember that she was no longer a cowering three-year-old, caught up in her mother's chaotic lifestyle, nor even a scared nine-year-old, terrified she would be taken from her grandparents. Back then, hiding had been her go-to strategy and she'd built dens wherever she could, cocooned herself away from the world.

But it really was not an option in the present situation, so she forced herself to stand tall and face him. Unfortunately, that necessitated looking at him, and her hormones did a flip before standing at attention.

Today Zander was suited and booted—the suit a faintly pinstriped charcoal grey, the shirt a pristine white. The whole ensemble epitomised wealth and success and a wow factor she really could do without. Dark blonde hair, just a little bit too long, blue-grey eyes that pierced... and suddenly the vast library seemed to shrink around her.

Eventually she located her vocal cords. 'What a surprise. Were you looking for me?' *Please let this be some strange coincidence.*

'Yes. You mentioned you worked as a university librarian—I did a bit of research and here I am.'

It occurred to her that despite the suave suit, he was uncomfortable; something in his expression indicated that the expensive shirt felt constrictive round his throat and the square jaw held a hint of tension.

'So, how can I help?'

'I was wondering if…if you'd have dinner with me.'

For a moment she couldn't hold back the instinct to smile. She felt a bubble of anticipation at the idea that their encounter had sparked this—a desire to follow up. Though something warned her that her reaction was misplaced and she dialled down the smile—an instinct justified by his next words.

'I've got a business proposition I want to discuss.'

Of course. How foolish of her to think it could be anything else. She could only hope he hadn't clocked her initial response. Especially idiotic because even if he *had* asked her on a date she would have refused. Zander was not her type—in so much as she *had* a type…which she didn't. But in the unlikely event that she ever figured out love and relationships she'd want someone ordinary, and Zander wasn't that. Being with Zander would be too much—too intense. He was too gorgeous, too rich, too successful…just too *everything*.

'You need a librarian?' Could he have a collection of books that needed cataloguing? It seemed unlikely.

'Nope.' He rubbed the back of his neck. 'It's complicated.'

The word should have her running for the sanctuary of her apartment. Gabby was a big fan of simplicity. Yet curiosity surfaced—what on earth could he have in mind? Hesitation stretched the silence and then she shrugged. After all, the point was that this wasn't a date—this was business.

So... 'OK. I'm intrigued. Dinner sounds good.'

'Great. Are you finished or shall we meet somewhere later?'

'I'm good to go.'

As they exited the university, Zander wondered if he had completely lost every vestige of common sense. Sitting at his desk earlier he had thought his idea made perfect sense, verging on genius. The problem was now he'd seen Gabby again he'd remembered the major flaw in the whole concept. In a nutshell—the Attraction Factor. One second in her presence was all it had taken for any ideas of business to desert him at supersonic speed. To be replaced by a near-overwhelming urge to cross the room and try for a repeat of that kiss.

But now, out in the fresh dusk-laden air, he sought perspective. Reminded himself that the attraction wasn't a problem as long as he didn't act on it.

'I thought we'd eat at Lothario's.'

One of Bath's most prestigious restaurants, it would provide a persuasive backdrop to explain his proposition. Yet she didn't look impressed; in fact she didn't even look enthusiastic.

'Unless you'd prefer somewhere else?'

'Actually, I would rather go somewhere more low-key, if that's OK with you.'

'Sure.' So much for the dazzling-her-into-acceptance plan.

'There's a really good pizza place not far from here. How about we go there?'

Ten minutes later they entered a small cosy Italian restaurant from which wafted out the tantalising aroma of tomato, garlic and a hint of oregano. Most of the tables were occupied with an eclectic mix of diners, and the low-lit room exuded a lively ambience without being loud. The tables were a mixture of sizes and shapes and were cheerfully hung with red tablecloths.

The chefs tossed pizza bases into the air with verve and pizzazz.

A waiter stepped forward, led them to a table without fuss and left them with a smile and the menus.

Gabby gave hers a perfunctory glance and placed it on the table. 'I already know what I'm having,' she explained. 'Artichokes, capers, goat's cheese and olives. I always have that.'

'Always?'

'Yup. I don't eat out often, so I like to know for sure that I'll enjoy it.'

'But maybe you could swap something out? Have extra mozzarella instead of capers? Ham instead of artichokes? Or why not try the special? You may find something you like better.'

Zander stopped at the sight of Gabby's frown. For Pete's sake. What was *wrong* with him? The answer was not one he liked: discomfort. This was the first time he'd gone out with a woman since Claudia's death and he was assailed by an onslaught of nerves.

Zander hauled in a breath, reminded himself that this was a business dinner and it was time to put things on to that footing. 'Sorry. I didn't mean to sound so didactic. Especially over pizza toppings.'

'Apology accepted.'

Zander checked the menu, focused on the words and realised the irony of his own criticism. As a child, restaurants had been a nightmare for him—unable to decode the menus, he had simply pointed randomly to items with a varied degree of success. Or requested a staple generic dish that he knew would be on the menu.

The waiter returned with a long wooden board that held bread and three slender bottles of olive oil. 'Rosemary, chilli and plain,' he explained, then took their order and departed.

As she helped herself, Gabby glanced across at him. 'So,' she said, 'I'm intrigued. To be honest, I can't imagine what kind of business you have in mind.'

A sudden heat touched her cheekbones and she looked down at the piece of bread she held. A flash of insight told him with complete certainty that she had suddenly been hit with exactly the sort of business he currently had in mind.

Say something, Zander. Before the silence stretches so taut it snaps.

'Before we go any further, I need to know if you are in a relationship.'

'I can't see how that could possibly pertain to a business proposition.'

Her voice had a definite chill factor and he couldn't blame her.

'Humour me. Please. Just a simple yes or no will suffice. Then I'll explain.'

Gabby narrowed her eyes but then shrugged. 'No.'

Out-of-all-proportion relief touched him that his assumption had been correct. It was an assumption based purely on the sheer intensity of the kiss they had shared. Somehow he'd been sure that if Gabby was seeing someone, she wouldn't have kissed him like that.

'So explain,' she said flatly.

'It all started with that kiss. There were some rather unfortunate repercussions.'

The waiter reappeared with their wine, and the interlude gave him time to gather his thoughts and marshal them into coherence.

She tilted her head, waited for him to continue.

'You know my circumstances?'

'Sure. You run a highly successful consultancy company, with offices in London, Germany and

Ireland, you made your first million by the time you were twenty-seven, and you started your business from a rented garage whilst you slept in an ancient caravan because you gambled everything.'

Guilt delivered another sucker punch. He'd done all of that. His wife had died and it had kick-started his route to a success she would never see—a success that would not have happened had she lived.

It's not that I don't believe in you, Zan. It's just not worth the risk. What's wrong with what we have now? If you do something like that, I'll never see you. I want us to be together, have a family, not risk losing the roof over our heads.

Claudia's words were so clear in his head, but there was no point pursuing that path. Right or wrong, he'd done what he'd done.

'All that is correct,' he said. 'But I meant my personal circumstances.' Though he couldn't blame Gabby for citing his business ones. This was supposed to be all about business.

'I know that you were widowed. And as I said on Saturday I'm so very sorry. You must have been devastated.'

How to explain it? Explain that he had been

blasted with grief—grief at the loss of a life so young, grief that the girl he'd fallen in love with aged sixteen should have been taken, grief at the waste, the sadness, the sheer horror of watching someone you cared about fight and lose, slowly get weaker and fade away.

'It was difficult,' he said.

He waited as their pizzas arrived, black pepper and parmesan were dispensed. Then he continued, aware of the intent concentration of her expression, grateful for the lack of question or comment. Gabby was letting him tell the story as he wanted.

'Since Claudia's death I haven't had another relationship, and to be honest I am good with that. I haven't wanted one and I still don't. However, my family have different ideas. They are worried about me, think I need to move forward… and they spend way too much of their time trying to set me up.' He paused to sample the pizza and nodded. 'You're right. This is incredible.'

'Glad you like it.' She paused to pour chilli oil over her pizza. 'It's nice that your family cares.'

For a second he saw wistfulness cross her face.

'Yes. But on Saturday, after our…encounter, I

went back to Mum and Dad's and everyone fell on me with joy.'

'Why?'

He sighed. 'We were spotted by one of my mum's friends. Edna Harris, if you want to know full details.' The woman had an uncanny ability to nose out secrets, to be in the 'right' place at the 'right' time. 'She headed straight for Casa Grosvenor to share the glad tidings and my family are thrilled.'

Gabby's face held bemusement. 'OK. But I'm still not seeing this. All you had to do was explain you were helping out an old schoolmate with a hen challenge. End of.'

'Given the detail Edna went into about what she saw, it would have been a tricky explanation.'

Gabby speared an artichoke heart and shook her head. 'Yes, but...'

'You're right. I could have explained it. I decided not to.'

'Because...?'

The artichoke was halted, halfway to her mouth, and for a moment his gaze snagged on her lips. He remembered their feel, the taste of her, the sheer unexpected passion and desire that kiss had evoked...

Deep breath. He decided he might as well go for it. 'Because I thought it would be a great idea to pretend you are my girlfriend.'

The artichoke heart fell from her fork.

'That's why I'm here. I want to hire you to be my fake girlfriend.'

CHAPTER THREE

GABBY WATCHED THE descent of the artichoke heart on to the tomato sauce of her pizza as her brain scrambled for a response to his words... questioned whether she could have heard them correctly. Perhaps this was Zander Grosvenor's idea of some sort of bizarre joke. Perhaps her tomato-splattering response was being recorded by an unseen camera. If so, the image could be labelled *The Personification of Stupefaction*. Or maybe she had misheard him?

Trying not to gibber, she surveyed his expression—outwardly calm, with a hint of tension in his jawline.

Eventually her brain decided on a single syllable. 'Why?' Immediate hindsight suggested a simple no would have been a better choice, followed by a rapid exit.

Zander sipped his wine, then placed the glass down, his fingers still around the base. For a second she studied his hand—its size, its strength, the very faint smattering of hair, the sturdiness of his wrist—and a funny little thrill shot through her.

Wrenching her gaze away, she looked up. 'Why would you want to hire a fake girlfriend? If you need a girlfriend, I'm pretty sure you could muster up a real one.' The man was gorgeous and loaded and—oh, God, had she just given him the wrong idea? 'Not me, obvs. But I'm sure there would be plenty of women who would go out with you for nothing.'

'I don't want a real girlfriend. I don't want a real relationship. Not right now.' The words *or ever* seemed to hover unspoken over the table, implicit in his tone, and Gabby could have kicked herself around the restaurant. The man was a widower, either still in love with his wife or not yet ready to move on. She'd been so inappropriately focused on his damn hand she'd lost the plot.

'I'm sorry, Zander. I didn't mean any disrespect to Claudia.'

'None taken.'

'But I still don't get why on earth you would want a pretend girlfriend.'

'Because it would make my family happy.'

His sigh contained exasperation, but affection and warmth, as well. 'They were genuinely so thrilled that I might have found someone.'

'Did Edna Harris mention the bunny suit?'

'Yup. But I don't think they would have cared if you were naked.'

Had he really said that? *Naked?* The two syllables resonated in the air, evoking images he quickly censored. *Move along.*

'My sisters were happy I'd lightened up and met someone "fun". My mum was happy I'd met *anyone*, because she's worried I'll never get over Claudia.'

Do you think you will? She bit back the question. None of her business. God knew she didn't like discussing her own personal circumstances, her own losses and how she'd dealt with them. So instead she picked up a piece of pizza and contemplated him over the rim.

'I get that you want to make your family happy.'

Hell, she'd do anything for her grandmother. *Anything at all.* The familiar twinge of intertwined love, guilt and worry twinged her nerves. Her grandparents had used up their pension, the equity in their house on her—the cost of bringing up a child as they'd entered their seventies had taken a huge financial toll on them. Then, when her grandfather had died, his pension had stopped.

And now... Well, Gabby squirrelled away as much of her salary as she could for the future that she knew was imminent—the time when her grandmother would need more and more help at home to retain her independence. A time when there might be no choice but to find a residential care home. After all, Lucille had turned ninety the previous month.

Gabby would be more than happy to move in with her grandmother right now, but Lucille flatly refused, informing her that she didn't need to be tied to an old lady—she needed to be living her life and enjoying her youth. Nothing would budge her.

'Gabby?'

'Sorry. The thing is that, however much you love your family, faking a relationship is a little extreme. Plus...surely it's wrong.'

'Wrong in what way?'

'Well, it's an outright lie, for a start. But it's not only a factual lie. It goes deeper. You want to make them believe that you're getting over

Claudia, that you're moving forward, when you aren't.'

'I *have* got over Claudia. In the sense that I am not still in love with her or her memory. But my family won't accept that—they want proof, and the only proof I can offer them is a girlfriend.'

Gabby shook her head. 'But if you're over her, why not open yourself up to the idea of a *real* relationship? With someone you really like as opposed to a virtual stranger whom you kissed to help her out.'

For a treacherous instant the kiss returned to her mind, replayed in full neon pink bunny-suited glory. And in that instant a small voice from the deep recesses of her brain screamed at her to shut up! Questioned why she was having some sort of moral, intellectual discussion about this. Hell, if this man wanted a fake girlfriend, so what? She should take the opportunity and run with it.

Run where? interjected the voice of reason. *Towards more kisses?* That would be plain stupid.

'My reasons for not wanting another relationship are personal. My objective here is to combat my family's worries. And, from an entirely selfish viewpoint, I'd like them to cease their matchmaking efforts, which, frankly, are driving me nuts.'

'But...it won't *work*.'

'Why not?'

'Because presumably you don't want to continue this fiction for ever. So what happens a few months down the line when we split up? They'll start worrying again. Even more than they are now. Because if you dump the fake girlfriend—FG for short—then they'll think it's because of Claudia. And if FG dumps *you*, they'll be worried that you're heartbroken. Lose-lose.'

'I've thought of that. I'd make it clear from the get-go that the relationship isn't serious for either of us. You *or* me. It'll be a bit of fun, an interlude...a first step on the relationship ladder.'

To her surprise she felt a pang of hurt at the implication that that was all she could be. *Get real, Gabby—talk about oversensitivity.* This was a fictional, hypothetical scenario. Yet the idea of playing the role of 'an interlude' didn't appeal. Shades of her childhood. To her mother she had been an unfortunate interlude, not a commitment.

Aware of his scrutiny, the small crease on

his forehead, she shook her head. 'There is no "us"—this is a hypothetical question about you and FG.'

He raised a hand in mock surrender. 'Fair enough. But I have thought this through. This fake relationship will be a fun, strings-free one. Me putting my toe back in the relationship waters with someone not after commitment. That way my family won't try to gather FG into their bosom, but they will feel happy I am "moving forward". They will also stop trying to set me up with every female of their acquaintance. Win-win. It *will* work. So I need a real fake girlfriend. I need *you*. All you have to do is attend a few events with me, some family functions, be seen with me for a few months… And, of course, I'll pay you. So what do you think?'

'I think it's mad and you're madder.'

Suddenly he smiled. 'So you'll do it, then?'

For a moment the smile literally rendered her speechless. The usual gravity of his face had lightened, his eyes seemed flecked with wicked charm, and for a moment she almost entered the bubble of insanity and agreed.

As if he sensed her hesitation, he said, 'Come on Gabby. It might even be fun.'

Fun. Still under the spell of that smile, her brain was exhibiting interest in the whole ridiculous idea. Perhaps it was a bit like the urge to poke an aching tooth or prod a bruise. Plus he'd said he would pay her—so in truth this would be a *job*, a business transaction, a chance to put away a little extra money for her grandmother.

'What sort of events?'

'My sister is getting married in a couple of months in Bath—at the actual Roman Baths. And I'm hosting a charity gala next week in London. We'll need to have a few meals out, or other date-like activities in between. Smile for a few photos. There may be an interview or a few questions from reporters.'

The last words were said in such a casual tone that at first she didn't comprehend their meaning. And then suddenly a whole lot of dots were joined up. 'Exactly *who* is your sister marrying?'

'Alessio Bravanti.'

'The racing driver?' Just to be absolutely sure.

'That's the one.'

'And this charity gala—you don't mean a knees-up in the village hall? You're talking a full-on function? The type covered in celeb magazines?'

'Yes.' He eyed her, no doubt noting the horror that etched her features. 'Is that a problem?'

'Yes. I'm sorry, but you've got the wrong girl—the wrong candidate for the role.' Pushing her plate away, she shook her head, aware of a pulse of frustration-tinged regret. 'I wish I was the sort of woman who would jump at this, but I'm not. The whole thought of being watched and judged makes me come up in hives.'

'No one will judge you.'

'That's not true and you know it. Your family will definitely judge me, and I won't blame them for that. They care about you. But it won't only be them. What about all the guests at the wedding and the charity function? The reporters...the public...?'

'Why does it matter what they think?'

'Because words can hurt just as much as sticks and stones, and the wounds can take longer to heal.'

Gabby could still feel the pain she'd felt when her mother had been discussing her with her boyfriend du jour.

Yes, the kid's a pain...a drag. I know. I'll see if I can dump her with my parents again.

That sting would always be with her—the

knowledge that she was nothing more than an encumbrance.

'And people's opinions *do* matter.'

Sometimes they could even be life-changing. Social workers had watched her throughout her childhood, assessed her, assessed her grandparents, formed opinions, and Gabby had made damn sure she'd conformed to whatever they wanted.

She had been the child they'd needed her to be: quiet, invisible, polite, grateful… Whatever it took to jump the regulation hurdles and stay with her grandparents after her mother's death from an overdose. And she was still that person—the kind who shunned the limelight, the one who had never wanted to be anything like the 'party girl' her mother had been, the one who just wanted an ordinary life.

'So I'm sorry, Zander, but I can't do this. It wouldn't work.'

Perhaps she was mad, given that he would pay her and she would love the chance to add to her savings. But it wouldn't be fair to either of them when she knew she couldn't pull it off.

'I'm not the type of person who could act as your girlfriend—someone who goes to glittering events on the arm of a multimillionaire. You'll have to find someone else.' He opened his mouth and quickly she stood up. 'Bathroom break,' she said.

And on the way to the bathroom she'd pay the bill, say goodbye and leave. Because for some daft reason she felt bad—bad that she was refusing the job and bad that she was too chicken to take on a role that most people would kill for. But she knew it was the right decision. Gabby knew her limitations and this was definitely one of them. This role was beyond her abilities.

Five minutes later Zander watched as Gabby headed back to the table, her stride purposeful, the doubts he'd sensed earlier clearly dispelled. This was a woman on a mission to say farewell and leave as soon as possible. *Well, tough.*

She halted, looked down and frowned.

'I ordered dessert,' he explained. 'It's the house special, and according to the staff it's what you always have.'

The frown deepened. 'I… How on earth do they remember that?'

Her surprise was genuine, and Zander realised that Gabby really had no idea how memorable she was. He wasn't sure he could put his finger on it himself. She was undoubtedly pretty, but it went deeper than that. Perhaps it was the depth of expression in her hazel eyes, a sense of vulnerability...some elusive facet that etched her on people's memory banks.

'Anyway, I wasn't planning on staying.'

'But it would be a shame to waste it,' he said smoothly. 'And also I didn't have a chance to mention an important part of my proposition.'

There was a hesitation and then she sighed and sat down, picking up her spoon with an expression that indicated a determination to speed eat her way through the tiramisu.

'I didn't mention the fee.'

Now she looked up. 'The fee is irrelevant—because I'm not applying for the role.'

'I understand that, but if you were to agree to this I'm willing to pay you one hundred thousand pounds plus expenses.'

The spoon clattered to the table. 'Are you *nuts*?'

'Nope.'

'I guarantee you can get someone a lot cheaper than that.'

'I don't want someone else. I want you.'

Silence stretched taut as awareness joined the party—an awareness that swirled itself around them as he realised the truth of the words. He did want her. Right now he wanted to lean across the table and kiss her, taste the chocolate on her lips, entwine his fingers in the glossy sheen of chestnut hair, and then he wanted to…

Stop!

'You are the obvious choice.' The words sounded forced, his voice hoarse, and he picked up his espresso. 'You are the woman I kissed. The woman Edna saw.'

Gabby took her time replying, her cheeks still flushed as if she was able to read his mind. 'I doubt Edna could pick me out in an identity parade.'

'Maybe not, but I'd rather not risk it. I get that this isn't your sort of gig, but think what you could do with the money.'

A dreamy look entered her eyes and she caught her bottom lip between her teeth in clear indecision. Then, 'You're right. The money would be great. But I can't accept the job because it wouldn't be fair. I couldn't pull it off. It's not only the limelight factor.' Pushing her empty bowl away, she leant forward. 'In real life I wouldn't go out with you. So how on earth could I fake it? No one will believe it.'

To his surprise, chagrin punched his chest at her words. 'Why wouldn't you go out with me?'

'Does it matter?'

'Yes. Because if you tell me then I can work out if we can overcome it or not.'

'For a start, I would never agree to a temporary, fun, strings-free relationship.'

'Because you're looking for a happy-ever-after?' Try as he might he couldn't keep the wariness from his voice.

She reached out to cover his arm in an instinctive gesture of comfort. 'I'm sorry. I know your happy-ever-after ended in tragedy, and I understand why you may want a temporary relationship, but I… I still want a shot at it. One day.'

'So you won't embark on any relationship unless it's with Mr Right?'

'Let's say I don't want to embark on a deliberate relationship with someone who is definitely Mr *Wrong*.'

'Fair enough. But you wouldn't be. This would be a fake relationship.'

'But I would find it hard to maintain a pretence that goes against my character and my beliefs. That's hardly going to be easy to pull off, especially when I will be so far out of my depth I'll be in constant danger of drowning. You're a "catch." I'm ordinary and my ideal man is ordinary. You aren't that.'

A dark memory crossed his soul. Again Claudia's voice echoed in his imagination.

Why can't you be happy with what we have, Zan? With what you *have? Be happy to be ordinary instead of striving after an extraordinary dream that may ruin us.*

As she studied his expression Gabby shook her head. 'I didn't mean it as an insult. I just want to explain why you aren't my type.'

He couldn't let her get away with that. 'Don't you remember that kiss?'

Her lips parted and he wondered if she'd have the gall to deny any memory, to say *What kiss?* But instead, she shook her hair forward slightly to hide her face.

'Of course I do. But that didn't mean anything. It was just an anomaly.'

'Then why don't we try it again?'

'Excuse me?'

'You heard me.' Zander wasn't a hundred percent sure where he was going with this but... 'Why don't we try it again? Another kiss?'

'That is a ridiculous idea.'

'No, it isn't. Because *I* don't think it *was* an anomaly. On a physical level I think I *am* your type, and I know you're mine. And that is exactly why we can pull this off.'

'Relationships are about more than the physical.'

'Sure. But without a physical attraction there is no relationship. And in the case of a fun-filled interlude the physical aspect is the most important.'

'I am not kissing you *now*.' Gabby glanced around, then narrowed her eyes at him. 'I bring my *grandma* here, for goodness' sake.' Her forehead scrunched into a scowl. 'In fact I am not kissing you ever. If you think you can pay me to—'

'No!' How could he, Zander Grosvenor, king of the boardroom, dealmaker extraordinaire, be making such a hash of this? 'That isn't what I meant. I don't want to have a *real* physical relationship with you.'

Liar, liar, whole suit on fire!

Deep breath. 'I just want to demonstrate that whether we like it or not, act on it or not, there is a real physical attraction between us—and that means I think we could pull this off. Convince everyone that we are in a real relationship. Even though we won't be. On any level.' He leant back. 'Can you look me in the eye and tell me this attraction is a figment of my imagination?'

Against all odds her eyes scrunched further shut, and then she expelled a sigh. 'I can't do that. But believe me, I wish I could.'

Bingo! 'Then I respect your reservations, and I appreciate your honesty, but I believe we *can* do this. If I'm wrong that's my bad—not yours. So what do you think? A few social events and you pocket a hundred grand?'

Indecision hovered on her face, etched her forehead with a crease. She closed her eyes as if picturing the cash.

Finally she opened them and gave a small, decisive nod. 'OK. I'll do it. But only if I can tell my grandmother the truth.'

Zander hesitated.

'She won't tell a soul. I give you my word. Also, it's a non-negotiable condition.'

'Then so be it. You can tell your grandmother. Now, do we have a deal?'

'We have a deal.'

CHAPTER FOUR

'SO THAT'S HOW I made a deal with Zander Grosvenor.' Gabby summoned reassurance and a smile as she came to the end of her edited explanation to her grandmother.

Lucille had interspersed the recital with questions aplenty, and now her expression tended more towards dubious than joyful. 'I don't like it, Gabby. I especially don't like it that you are doing this for money to look after *me*.'

Gabby grinned. 'So if I was doing it for money for me, that would be all right?'

'It would be better!' Lucille settled back on the chair and tucked her shawl over her knees.

'It's not exactly a hardship. Most women would volunteer for the job, forget getting paid for it!'

'You aren't "most women" and I am sure you have no wish to have a temporary fling with a man just because he is good-looking and rich.'

'But I'm *not* having a fling with him, Gran. I'm *pretending* to.'

'Gabrielle. I may be old, but I am not stupid. I understand that this is a pretence. But it isn't one I approve of. It's a lie, and it's a lie you won't enjoy enacting. A gentleman wouldn't ask you to do that.'

'But his motivations are good.'

'Would your granddad have liked him?'

'Yes.' The answer came from her gut, even though she wasn't sure where the conviction came from. 'He married his childhood sweetheart and he has remained loyal to her memory. He loves his family enough to concoct an illusion, possibly *delusion*, of a relationship for them.'

Lucille shook her head, her still bright blue eyes clouded with trouble. 'It seems to me he'd be better to face his family head-on.' Sadness touched her features. 'Though what do *I* know about family relationships?'

'Don't say that, Gran.' Gabby knew that Lucille still grieved for her daughter—would always blame herself for the path Karen had taken. That was why, all her life, Gabby had striven to be the polar opposite of her mother. 'You and

Gramps understood all about relationships, and I couldn't have asked for more caring people to bring me up.'

'Thank you, darling.' For a second she smiled, then took Gabby's hand and squeezed gently. 'Promise me you'll be careful.'

Sensing her grandmother was tired, Gabby nodded. 'I promise.'

'Don't get your heart broken. He's a good-looking, charming, successful man.'

'He may be all those things, but Zander Grosvenor is not my type at all. In the slightest.'

Lucille raised one delicately pencilled brow and Gabby reminded herself that she had down-played the kiss and utterly omitted even a mention of any attraction.

'I'm in this for the money and I am in no danger at all of falling for the boss!'

The words were nothing but the truth. The attraction was an annoyance, an irritation, a problem she intended to solve. Even if she hadn't figured out how yet.

And perhaps her scowl carried conviction, because Lucille nodded. 'OK. Then enjoy yourself, darling.'

Yeah, right. The prospect of the next weeks

showed a vista that crossed so far into her discomfort zone her eyes crossed at the mere thought. But she wouldn't add to Lucille's worry by sharing that.

'I will—and I will give you regular updates as to my progress. Right now I'm off to meet Zander to sort out the small print. We're going boating on the river...'

Fifteen minutes later, Gabby approached the boat hire company based on the banks of the River Avon. It had seemed a suitable date-like activity, and Zander had pointed out they could speak without fear of being overheard in a boat. As a bonus, she sincerely hoped open air and wide outdoor spaces would act as a deterrent to their attraction.

It was a hope that lasted precisely as long as it took for her to spot Zander. As he rose from the riverside bench her tummy flipped. He was dressed in stonewashed jeans, a white T-shirt and trainers. The simple outfit showcased his sheer masculinity, the hard curve of his muscles, and threw her hormones into disarray. Yet she forced her feet to maintain pace as she walked towards him.

'Hey.'

His voice rippled over her skin as he stepped forward, his hands outstretched.

'Hey.' Belatedly she realised that they were now in role. She placed her hands in his and her skin goosebumped despite the warmth of the late-spring sunshine. 'Are we being watched?'

'Let's say I wouldn't put it past any of my family to be lurking behind a tree somewhere.'

'So you told them?'

At least her voice appeared to work, even though every one of her senses was focused on the strength of his grip, the feel of his skin against hers.

'Yes…' Zander, too, seemed mesmerised by their clasped fingers, until in an abrupt movement he dropped her hand. 'So it's probably best if we continue this conversation once we are on the river.'

'Good plan.'

It was an activity to focus on, and for a moment she did exactly that. Studied the row of wooden boats bobbing on the water—punts, skiffs and canoes.

'Which one shall we hire?'

'A skiff. I'm happy to row, or we can take turns.'

'You go first and then I'll try, depending on how easy it is. I don't want to capsize.'

Ten minutes later they climbed on to a long, varnished wooden boat and Gabby could see the owner had been right. The graceful slender craft was built for speed, but was also wide enough for stability and comfort.

Zander sat in the centre, an oar in each hand, and she settled herself against the traditional wicker backrest and tried to visualise the instructions they had been given. 'So I can help steer by using these lines?'

'Yup. They're connected to the rudder. But don't worry about it too much. When I came here with my sisters, their attempts at steering nearly capsized us.'

'Hmm… Well, I'll do my best—though, to be honest, I'm quite happy to just keep a lookout for otters.'

In reality, for the next five minutes, her gaze was focused exclusively on observing Zander row, watching the flex of his muscular forearms, the strength and sculpt of his biceps. She tried to tell herself that her entrancement was due to the necessity for study, for learning the technique for when she came to take the oars herself. She knew that theory held not an iota of truth—she could only hope she wasn't drooling.

Enough. Time to recall exactly why they were here. 'So, how did your family take the news about "us"?'

'They were all thrilled.'

Try as she might, she couldn't interpret either his expression or his tone—relief, ruefulness, regret or all three? 'That's good, right?'

'Yes. They are happy, and they have abandoned their plans to hook me up with every female of their acquaintance.'

'I sense a *but.*'

'Not a *but,* exactly. More of a realisation that I've rolled the dice and the game has begun. Now it is imperative that we make this work.'

'Yes.'

Gabby could hear the fervour in her own voice. After all, she knew how it felt to build up a fantasy world that collapsed about you in a rubble of disillusionment. When she had been small, and her mother had constantly left her with her grandparents, appearing and reappearing in her life with bewildering uncertainty, Gabby hadn't understood why.

Her grandparents had wanted to spare her pain and so had allowed Gabby to believe in the scenarios she'd created. That her mother was ill but missed her so very much. Or was away working somewhere where children weren't allowed. Occasionally her imagination went into fantastical overdrive and she made her mother a princess, a mermaid…

Eventually, though, the bubble had burst, and the grim reality of the time she spent with her mother—the dirt, the grime, the empty alcohol bottles and drug paraphernalia—were all things she couldn't weave into her fantasies. So she'd confronted her grandparents and forced them to tell her the truth. It had truly shattered her world. Made her feel stupid, angry and sad, and hurt by the deceit. The feelings had been made all the worse because she hadn't been able to express them to her grandparents, afraid she would lose them, too.

'Gabby?'

'Sorry.' Gabby tried to push away the onslaught of qualms and concentrated on the swish of the oars in the water. This illusion bore no similarity to those of her childhood. Yet… 'Are you sure about this, Zander? Maybe you should come clean now. Before this goes further. If they find out, they'll feel hurt and stupid.'

For a second he hesitated, his dark eyes serious as he considered her words, and then he shook his head. 'No. The die is cast. Now we need to play our parts with conviction.'

'Then let's get to work. If we want to make this believable, the detail is important. We have to fabricate this so well that *we* almost believe it's true.'

That was a fact. Sometimes she even wondered if her whole personality was based on a part she had played for so long that it had become the truth.

'What exactly did you tell your family about me? I need to figure out what they're expecting.'

'I said I bumped into you in town, remembered you from school. We got chatting, had a coffee and things went from there. I said that we both agree we're not looking for anything serious, just some uncomplicated fun. Mum and Dad are pleased. Julia is worried you're after my money—that you staged the meeting—and

Gemma hopes it will turn serious. That's because Julia is a cynic and Gemma is a romantic.'

'Great. So Julia will check my bag for a gold-digging shovel and Gemma will expect me to fall at your feet adoringly.'

'Nope. I sorted it. I told them neither scenario is the truth—that you aren't after my wallet or my heart, just my body.'

Gabby closed her eyes in silent horror.

'And I wiggled my eyebrows.'

'Suggestively, no doubt? So they now think I'll rip your clothes off in public?'

Nice one, Gabs. With any luck she'd be tipped overboard and get swallowed up by the depths of the river.

'You could try it and see.'

Was he laughing at her? *Yup.* Her mortification had triggered an upward quirk of his lips and his eyes had a wicked glint that turned her knees wobbly.

'In your dreams!'

'Probably,' he agreed, and her cheeks heated as she narrowed her eyes at him.

'You need to take this seriously!'

Yet it wasn't possible not to smile back, not to revel in the flirtatious undertones, the shimmer of attraction that vested their conversation with a thrill.

'I am. This is part of getting in character—you said we need to almost believe it ourselves. Two people in a fun, flirty relationship where we kick back and enjoy ourselves. Have a bit of banter. That's what a fun fling is all about, isn't it?'

'I wouldn't know.' To her own irritation she could hear wistfulness in her voice.

His lips twisted ruefully. 'Neither would I.'

Realisation dawned on her that he wouldn't. This guy was a one-woman man, and that in itself sent a cascade of emotion through her, a glow not of desire but warmth. *Stop!* Lust was bad enough. Warmth was not an affordable emotion.

Before she could stop herself she asked, 'So since Claudia you really haven't dated anyone? Or seen anyone? Or...done anything with anyone?' *Very subtle, Gabs.*

'No, I haven't.' He leant the oars against the side of the boat, that amused glint back in his eyes. 'If you're asking what I think you're asking—no, I haven't. Slept with anyone.'

'Oh.'

Gabby *knew* she should leave it, but she was having a little difficulty with the whole concept.

'I understand that you loved Claudia very much and you want to remain faithful to her memory...'

The boat jolted as Zander resumed rowing, his actions jerkier than before, the amused glint vanished.

'But surely you don't plan to remain celibate all your life? I mean, *why* haven't you had a fun fling? For real? Or a one-night stand?'

For a moment she wasn't sure he'd answer, wasn't sure she should have asked. Then he shrugged.

'I've been busy. These past five years I've put all my energy into my business. It hasn't been a deliberate choice as such to avoid women, but I haven't had the time or the inclination to indulge in any sort of a relationship.'

The word was said as if it were a contagious disease rather than an indulgence.

'So that's me. What about you? I gather you aren't a fan of fun flings. But what about past relationships?'

Damn. Now she really regretted asking him

anything, because she could hardly refuse to reciprocate. Though she could at least prevaricate…

'My turn to row, I think.'

'Sure.'

It was only then that she realised her mistake, because now they had to swap places, manoeuvre past each other. Rising, she tried to steady herself as the skiff bobbed on the water, and for a moment she wondered if she'd topple over. Then, in one lithe movement, Zander stood up, somehow balanced his weight so that the skiff itself seemed to steady, and his hands were on her waist, steadying her.

Chill, Gabby.

Zander was holding her for practical reasons, to help her get her balance. But, *hell*, it didn't feel like that. Her body's reaction was downright *personal*, and the cotton of her T-shirt was a flimsy barrier as they carefully edged their way round in a circle, their bodies close. Her heartbeat echoed in her ears. It was a Herculean effort not to close the gap between them.

Finally he released her, and she lowered herself into the vacated seat and picked up the oars. She watched the ripples in the water and glanced at the trees that fringed the lake, their branches swaying in the slight breeze, the different shades of green redolent of new beginnings and growth. She looked anywhere but at Zander until she had her breathing back under control.

'Right. Past relationships. There are two. Steve and Miles. Neither worked out.'

Sometimes she still wasn't sure why. It was as though at some point someone had handed out a rule book when she hadn't been there and no one had bothered to send it to her. No matter how hard she tried she hadn't been able to figure out how to play her part right, and the harder she'd tried, the more clingy and insecure she'd become.

Both Steve and Miles had been good, solid, ordinary blokes, and both had ended the relationship, citing the whole "it's not you, it's me" argument, having met someone else. Steve had explained that when he'd met his new love there had been a spark that had been lacking with Gabby. Miles had used terminology such as 'fizzled out'. Gabby was no fool and she could spot a pattern—in the context of relationship fireworks, she was a damp squib. So she had decided to leave the display and opt for singledom.

'So I've put relationships on hold.' Until maybe someday when that rule book arrived.

'So for you a fun fling would be out of the question on principle?'

Well, didn't *that* make her sound boring? And suddenly for a minute, as the sun glinted on the water and the sound of the oars swished in her ears, she wished she could throw caution to the wind and be the sort of person who could kick back and enjoy herself.

'It's not a principle. It just doesn't work for me.' Her mum had seen parenting as a short-term, temporary thing. Had worshipped at the altar of fun. 'Short-term makes me feel like I'm not up to scratch. Not good enough to be permanent.'

Even as she said the words she regretted them—better to be judged boring than pathetic.

'Not me personally,' she added. 'I mean in general.'

The slight quirk of his eyebrow indicated doubt. 'But surely that is only if the fling isn't on equal terms? If you want it to be more permanent and the other person doesn't then, yes, I get that. But if you *both* agree you want something temporary then that isn't a judgement on either of you.'

'I guess I just don't *do* temporary.' There had been way too much of that in her life. Temporary stints with her mother, temporary stays with her grandparents. The fear of going into temporary care. As far as she was concerned, temporary sucked, and it smacked of not being good enough. After all, she hadn't been good enough for her mum to change her lifestyle.

'Whoa! Slow down, Gabby.'

Huh?

'Oh.' Belatedly she realised that she was moving them along at breakneck speed. Worse, there was a boat headed towards them and she seemed to have rowed straight on to a collision course. 'Sorry.'

Zander steered and she rowed and, to her relief, the two crafts squeaked past each other without mishap.

'You OK?'

'I'm fine.' But it was time to get back on track. 'Anyway, it's going to be really hard to get *anyone* to believe either of us is up for a fun fling, let alone your family. So we need to get down to the nitty-gritty detail.' She glanced round the boat. 'I need to take notes, so perhaps we should stop at a riverside pub and see if we can find a secluded corner...'

CHAPTER FIVE

TWENTY MINUTES LATER Zander handed Gabby the orange juice she'd requested and seated himself opposite her in the shade of a willow tree in a corner of the pub garden.

'Right...'

As she pushed a stray tendril of glossy hair away she looked endearingly pretty, and he squashed the urge to lean over and tuck another escaped strand behind her ear.

'First, tell me about this charity event.'

'Its aim is to raise funds for a dyslexia awareness charity, and help promote the need for early recognition in schools.'

'I see.' But both her frown and her tone indicated surprise. 'I assumed that it would be connected to Claudia?'

Zander shook his head. 'I donate privately to a cancer charity and I have set up a medical scholarship in Claudia's name.'

Of course he had considered hosting fundraisers in Claudia's memory, but in truth he'd bottled it. Unable to face the sympathy, the need to relive those last months of her life, the complexities of his emotions around his marriage and her death.

'So why dyslexia?'

'Because, whilst it isn't a life-threatening illness, its impact can be devastating.'

Her hazel eyes surveyed him. 'That sounds like a knowledge born of experience.'

'It is. I'm dyslexic. I was diagnosed very late, and for a long time I believed I was stupid.'

His stomach hollowed in memory of the awful gnaw in its pit as his childhood self had stared at the jumble of shapes in front of him, desperately trying to rearrange them, to work out what they meant. Of the shameful, humiliating knowledge that around him everyone else could do it. Could see it. Could manage it. Could read and write. But he couldn't.

'I'm sorry.'

Sincerity shone from her eyes and he suspected his attempt at a neutral expression and factual tone had backfired.

'I'm not dyslexic, so I can't understand how that feels and I won't pretend to understand. But I *do* know how it feels to believe you're stupid, and it sucks. For a variety of reasons I missed a lot of school, and by the time my attendance became regular I was far behind everyone else. I dreaded every lesson, knew my ignorance would be exposed. In the end my grandparents paid for a private tutor and I caught up. I know it's not the same, but I know it must have been tough for you.'

He sensed she didn't usually share this information, and without thought he reached out and covered her hand in his. 'It sounds like it was tough for us both.'

Her proximity, the softness of her hand under his, the slenderness of her wrist, the warmth in her eyes, the almost impossible length of her eyelashes, the curve of her lips all combined to throw him for a loop.

Focus. Under the pretext of drinking his coffee, he lifted his hand from hers.

As if that had broken the spell, she frowned. 'How old were you when you were diagnosed? I don't remember you being dyslexic at school. I *do* remember you being cool and popular.'

'I worked at it. And I made sure I excelled at sports.'

He had been on every possible school team.

Plus, over the years he'd learnt to mask his dyslexia—persuaded friends to write his essays, made out he didn't care that he was failing, messed around in class to be cool, figured out ways to slip under the radar.

'And then I got lucky. When I was seventeen, at college, with hardly any GCSEs to my name, my football coach figured it out—and I got diagnosed with dyslexia. Late, but not too late. Not everyone is so lucky.'

Enough of his life story.

'So I thought I'd organise a fundraiser. My family have all pitched in to help. Alessio can't be there, as he has an event, but he has donated his yacht as the venue. The tickets have all been purchased. There will be an auction and a four-course dinner, music and dancing, and *Glossip* is writing it up.'

He'd swear she'd turned a greyish shade of pale, but she gave a small determined nod.

'I'll do my best to play my part. Could you let me have a copy of the guest list?'

'No problem.'

'And could you tell me more about your family? Just some background and a quick character sketch.'

'My mum was a nurse. She retired a couple of years ago. She always said she would have loved to be a doctor, but her family didn't support that. She had a difficult start in life, and as a result she wasn't in a position to get into medical school. My dad is an electrician, also retired, and has discovered a late-life interest and talent for golf. There wasn't a lot of money when I was growing up, but there was a lot of encouragement and heaps of expectation. My sisters thrived—Julia is a human rights lawyer and Gemma is a surgeon.'

Gabby looked slightly daunted and he couldn't blame her. As a child that was how *he'd* felt. Two high-achieving siblings and then there was Zander. The Failure.

'We grew up in Bath and my parents still live here. Julia, Gemma and I all live and work in London, but we come back to visit often. Julia is divorced with two kids, and somehow manages to juggle everything because she's scarily efficient. Gemma is the one getting married in a few weeks. She's very career-oriented and we didn't think she would ever want to settle down. Then Alessio swept her off her feet.'

'He's your best friend, right? Does that bother you? Your best mate and your sister?'

'Nope.'

In truth, it terrified him, because he no longer believed in happy-ever-after. He knew with bone-deep certainty that people changed, that love could wither away. But it was an opinion he couldn't share. Not without bursting the illusory bubble of his own happy-ever-after. The only consolation was that at least Claudia had never suspected his doubts, his frustration, the cold, growing realisation that he had made a mistake. He didn't want that for his friend or his sister; hoped it wouldn't happen to them.

'I'm happy for them.'

Expression intent, Gabby scribbled in her notebook, her handwriting a series of loops and generous curves. 'Tell me a bit about your sister's children.'

'Freddy is seven and Heidi is five, and they're small balls of energy who never stop talking and are interested in everything. I looked after them for a weekend last month and by the end of it I was a wreck. Good for nothing but a cup of cocoa and a nine o'clock bedtime.'

He could hear the affection in his own voice, and clearly so could Gabby.

'Sounds like you're a great uncle. You're lucky.

Your family sounds amazing.' The wistfulness in her voice was unmistakable.

'They are.' Zander hesitated and then continued. 'What about you? Are you an only child? I don't know the details, but at school Claudia did mention that you lived with your grandparents.'

'Yes.' Her voice was flat. 'My parents died. My grandparents were wonderful and they agreed to take me on. They were brilliant. Truly brilliant. At the time Gran was seventy and Gramps was seventy-two. It would have been completely understandable if they had decided it was too much. Instead they gave me security and love. I owe them a great deal. Gramps died several years ago. I still miss him, but obviously Gran was devastated. They were married for over sixty-five years.' Her voice was soft now, and a look of admiration touched with sorrow filled her eyes. 'They married when Gran was nineteen and Gramps was twenty-one. How incredible is that?'

'That *is* incredible.'

Sadness touched him now—at the knowledge that it was possible to grow old together, to marry young but make it through. But not for him. He knew that now. Because he was governed by an ambition that took precedence over everything and everyone—even now, when he had achieved so much, he wanted more. To grow the business, make it global, show everyone that he was the best. That was his priority, and he *knew* any relationship couldn't compete.

'I'm sorry.' Her voice was soft. 'I didn't mean to remind you of the chance you lost.' She hesitated. 'I asked Gran once whether if Gramps had died younger there could have been anyone else.'

'What did she say?'

'She said yes. She said that even now, aged ninety, she wouldn't ever discount the chance to love. She said that it would have been a different love, because it would have been with a different person, but that love is always worth having. That if she had gone first she would have wanted Gramps to be happy and would have hoped he'd find love again.'

'I understand that. For me, though, I am truly happier on my own. Not because I disagree with your gran, but because I am a different person now and a relationship is no longer what I want.'

'For ever? What about children? The way you spoke about Freddy and Heidi… You clearly love them.'

'I do. But that doesn't make me good father material.'

That was an absolute. Claudia had wanted children but Zander had prevaricated. Had put his business ambitions first. With the result that Claudia had missed out on motherhood.

'I am a self-confessed workaholic. There's no point having a family you never see.'

Time to shift focus away from him; this wasn't a discussion he wanted to get into.

'What about you? Do you want the whole package? Mr Right and 2.4 kids? With a white picket fence thrown in?'

'Yes. I do want children. But only with Mr Right. I know there is no guarantee of either, but that's my aim. If I have children I want to believe I can give them everything. Security, love, a brilliant dad and a stable family life.'

Further evidence, if any were needed, that he and Gabby were poles apart in their life goals.

Gabby blinked, picked up her pen and clicked the end. 'We seem to have got distracted.'

Zander shook his head. 'Not really. If we were really having a fun fling, we would have discussed all this. To make sure neither of us had false expectations of the other. I'd need you to know I'm not your Mr Right.'

'I think I'd have figured that out by now. So, now we need to convince everyone that we are Mr and Ms Right for Now but Not Right for Ever.' A smile curved her lips. 'It's not very catchy, is it?'

His gaze snagged on her mouth and he forced himself to focus on his coffee. He sipped it and almost welcomed the bitter coldness of the dregs. 'So what next?'

'I need to look the part. I have no idea what fun flings wear.'

'I don't think there is a dress code.' Seeing her hazel eyes cloud in genuine worry, he was aware that he wanted that smile back and clicked his fingers. 'I've got it! Get that bunny suit back and we're set. I'll even wear a matching pink bow tie and socks.'

Her eyes widened and he gave a sudden crack of laughter. 'If you could see your face! I'm not serious.'

'Thank goodness. But could you imagine it?' There was a moment of contemplation and then she gave a small, delicious gurgle of laughter.

'You could go for matching bunny ears. That would convince your family you'd gone bonkers.'

He had a sudden vision of his family's bemused expressions and joined in her laughter. When was the last time he'd laughed like this? Dammit—he couldn't remember.

Eventually she subsided, and worry shadowed those hazel eyes again. 'Seriously, though, I don't want to look wrong.'

'You won't.' And he meant it. Sitting opposite him, her make-up-free face touched by sunshine and laughter, her glossy chestnut hair gleaming and dappled, she looked beautiful. 'Whatever you wear you'll be...' *Beautiful.* 'Fine.'

'It's not that simple. I don't want to stand out... I—' Breaking off, she shook her head. 'Don't worry. This isn't your problem. I'll do some research and figure out how to fit in.' *Deep breath.* 'But it's not just about clothes. It's about how we act around each other. Should we be lovey-dovey? Hold hands and gaze at each other in adoration? Or opt for smouldering?'

Momentary panic touched him—a sudden realisation of what he had got himself into—and he could see the echo of anxiety cloud her eyes. The thought of love and adoration, even of the counterfeit variety, made him cringe. But it was too late for reservations now—the whole point of this charade was that it had to carry conviction.

'Option three is our best bet, I think. This is all about attraction.'

Now the clouds in her eyes stormed. 'You make it sound so easy. It isn't. When we walk on to this yacht peopled by celebrities and your family, no one will believe this. I could smoulder all I want—all that will happen is my dress will scorch. *No one* is going to buy this.'

Panic escalated in her voice, shone from her wide hazel eyes, and he recognised the signs of a person about to back out of a deal. 'Gabby? Slow down. Listen to me. I really don't think we'll have a problem. I could probably get people to invest in our smoulder factor.'

'You don't understand…'

'Maybe not. But I do understand this.'

Instinct took over and he twisted his chair to face her, angled himself into exactly the right position to lean forward and claim her lips.

A small gasp escaped her, and then without hesitation she pressed against him, her lips parted and her hands twined round his neck. Then he was lost, the last vestiges of common sense fled, and all he could think about was the moment, the vanilla scent of her hair that tickled his cheek with exquisite softness, the tang of citrus on her lips, the fierceness of his desire for her. For Gabby.

The intensity was too much—until the sound of laughter from a group of people as they sat down at a nearby table penetrated the fog, pulled him back to reality and the realisation that if they didn't stop he wouldn't be able to. Even so, pulling away was way harder than it should be, and the level of reluctance blared a klaxon of warning.

This was meant to be fake. The kiss was supposed to have been a tactical exercise to keep Gabby at the table, in the deal.

They sat for a moment and simply gazed at each other, until she gave a small half laugh followed by a muttered curse. 'I don't know what else to say. That was…'

'Awesome?'

'An awesome mistake.'

'Why?'

'Because neither of us wants to make this real.' She touched her lips as if in wonder. 'And that was real. A more important reality, though, is that you don't want the complication of any sort of relationship with anyone, and I'm—'

'Waiting for Mr Right.'

And she didn't do temporary. Both absolutely excellent reasons why that kiss should never have happened. Gabby had made it more than clear that she didn't want a purely physical relationship. She was holding out for the real thing. What her grandparents had had. What he knew he couldn't offer. Hell, what he didn't even *want* to offer. So...

'You're right. I shouldn't have kissed you.'

Yet it was nigh on impossible for him to regret it.

'Hey. There are two of us at the table. But it can't happen again.'

'You're right. No more kisses.' A nascent emotion that he knew to be regret surfaced and he pushed it down. 'But we will have to play our parts, and that will necessitate a certain level of closeness.' *Heaven help him.*

'I understand that.'

Somehow he had to get this back on to a business footing, because right now—*dammit*—he wanted to kiss her again. *Madness.*

'Then we're good to go. You need to give me

your bank details. This...arrangement...will continue until my sister's wedding in three months, so I'll pay you in three monthly instalments. I'll also set out a schedule of our dates, starting with the charity event on Friday.'

Gabby clicked her pen again, the sound a signal of her relief at the turn of the conversation. 'OK. Shall I meet you there?'

'No. Seeing as the gala is in London, it will be easier and look better if you come to my flat before. You can get ready there and stay the night after. I have two spare rooms you can choose from, which will make it less awkward than our staying in a hotel—if that's OK with you.'

The idea of Gabby in his apartment already felt heavy with awkward portent. The idea of *any* woman there filled him with unease; the idea of *Gabby* there gave him a severe case of the collywobbles.

And, although she nodded in agreement, the agitated *click-click-click* of her pen indicated that the collywobbles were mutual.

CHAPTER SIX

GABBY STOOD OUTSIDE the imposing block that overlooked the Thames—the whole edifice was ridiculously overwhelming. The thought of the combined worth of all the apartments made her eyes cross.

The butterflies that had occupied her tummy for the better part of the day swooped and dived. For most of the week she had toyed with the idea of backing out, all the while knowing she wouldn't. She couldn't walk away from the money for her grandmother's sake, and wouldn't renege on a deal for the sake of her own pride. Yet the knowledge that in a moment she would enter a penthouse apartment on the edge of the Thames, and would then attend a celebrity charity gala with Zander, felt madly surreal. Too much.

Her arm felt heavy as she buzzed for entry, then pushed the communal door open, entered the state-of-the-art lift and pressed the button for the sixth floor.

Seconds later the lift door opened and Zander stood outside, clad in jeans and a T-shirt, barefoot, his dark blonde hair shower-damp. Her heartbeat escalated.

'Hey.'

'Hey. Come on in.'

The words were polite, but she sensed a reluctance that matched her own as he led her to his flat and pushed open the heavy-looking door. Somehow the act of stepping over the threshold felt stupidly personal, an invasion of his privacy.

Shaking off the sensation—this was all Zander's idea, after all—she looked around with burgeoning curiosity. The hall stretched forward in its immensity, with rooms off to the sides. Yet it wasn't just the size she noted—it was the utter starkness of the decor, the swathes of beige on the wall not enlivened by a mirror, a picture—anything. The luxurious cream carpet ran clear, with hardly any furniture to impede its length.

'Would you like a cup of tea, coffee—something stronger?'

'No. Thank you.' Suddenly the sheer size of the apartment combined with his presence brought on a desire to escape. 'It's probably best if I go straight to get ready. I don't want to make us late.'

A quick nod of his head and he set off down the hall before pausing outside a door. 'Here you go.'

An hour later Gabby paced up and down the bedroom—the size at least allowed scope for long strides—and paused in front of the mirror. *Again.* Stared at her reflection. *Again.* Wondered whether she'd got this all wrong. *Again.*

Panic at the idea of all those guests—the rich and famous, the reporters from *Glossip*, the photographers and Zander's family—*everyone* watching her, twisted her insides. They would all see through her. They would know that she was an impostor. Especially in this dress. What had she been thinking?

Chill out. Hopefully the herbal remedy she'd taken to calm her anxiety would soon kick in. The concoction bought from her local health food shop had come highly recommended by a student who suffered from exam nerves, and Gabby had figured she might as well give it a try.

Resisting the urge to recommence the pacing,

she studied her image instead and started to talk herself off the ledge of anxiety, exactly as her childhood self had done.

First, she looked at her surroundings, focused on objects and decor—an exercise in grounding. The bedroom continued the beige theme, and the room was furnished as if from a tick list. Double bed, wardrobe, bedside cabinets. *The End*. The room had an unused feel to it, and she couldn't help but wonder if she was its first ever occupant.

Next she turned her attention back to her reflection. The dress was fine—it suited her and muted her, would hopefully allow her to fade away into the background. For better or worse, she'd decided to go the high-street route. She had visited the most exclusive boutique in Bath and been unable to justify the prices, despite the generous expenses allowance Zander had transferred into her account. She'd donated most of it to the dyslexia charity Zander was supporting.

In truth, it hadn't all been altruism—the thought of wearing one of those expensive designer dresses had brought the aphorism 'mutton dressed as lamb' to mind. Although she knew in theory she would fit in better if she wore the same sort of thing as the other guests, in reality she knew it wouldn't work like that—in some way she would still be recognised as an impostor. Better to remain true to herself, play the part of a temporary fling who didn't want to be dressed by her...lover.

Lover. The word brought the panic back in a waterfall of nerves, and she focused on the dress itself.

Black. Strapless. Long. Bodice boning ensured the top half contoured her curves. The satin skirt fell to the floor in a satisfying sweep and swish of elegance and modesty. Her hair fell in a simple curtain to her bare shoulders, her make-up was a study in the art of discretion.

Somehow she would get through the evening, pull off this nonsensical fantasy and *this time tomorrow it will all be over.* Plus, she had a new secondary mantra in place now—*think of the money.*

The reminder steadied her. Because at the end of the day, no matter what personal humiliation or social anxiety she had to endure, she'd get to walk away with enough money to ensure her grandmother would get the care she deserved. So she would hold nerves at bay and go and do the job she had agreed to do.

After all, she'd played a role before when the stakes had been way higher—the part of a well-adjusted child when she'd been an inner wreck. So this would be fine.

Yet the knock at the bedroom door triggered a further burst of butterflies, along with a stupid thrill of anticipation. *Ridiculous.*

She pulled the door open and stepped outside into the hall. The anticipation was justified—one look at him and all her brain could think was, *Yum.* Every instinct told her to use her arms to pull him up close and personal. Every instinct except the one of self-preservation. But Zander looked gorgeous—the tuxedo emphasised every lithe muscle, added a devil-may-care twist to his dark good looks, emphasised by the glint of his dark blonde hair.

The silence lengthened and she stepped backwards, reminding herself that they could not let physical attraction overcome common sense. And yet a deep yearning sparked inside her, curiosity as to what it would be like simply to succumb. To grasp the lapels of his tux, drag him towards her, kiss him senseless and pull him into the bedroom.

As if. That would be so far out of character that

she would suspect she'd been possessed. So instead she said, with a brightness that rung false, 'Hey!'

'Hey...'

It occurred to her that despite the aura of drop-dead gorgeousness he was nervous—acting as awkwardly as it was possible for Zander Grosvenor to be. *Oh, God.* Had he taken one look at her and realised what she'd been trying to tell him all along? That she couldn't cut the mustard—or any other condiment for that matter? That no one would believe this ridiculous charade?

'You look great,' he said eventually.

Yet she didn't believe him as he shifted his weight from foot to foot, his stance the epitome of discomfort. Was it her? She needed to know the truth.

'If I don't look right you need to tell me. We can't make this work if I look wrong.' If she was not a plausible date for Zander Grosvenor.

Zander frowned, gave his head a small shake and then he looked at her—properly looked at her—and her skin rippled with a shiver of desire.

'You don't look wrong. You look fantastic.' A small smile tipped his lips. 'I promise. This will work. We've *got* this.'

His voice deep, full of promise of a different type, and there it was again, that desire to close the gap and kiss him. But that way lay a road she would not walk—she could not be an interlude, a temporary rung on his ladder to getting over Claudia.

Claudia. The reminder was stark—and needed. 'Thank you. Now, we'd better go.'

We've got *this... We've* got *this... We've* got *this.*

As Zander drove with easy competence through the London streets Gabby concentrated on the role she would play. This was no different from her careful preparations before each social worker's visit, her daily preparations when she'd first moved in with her grandparents. She'd moulded herself a persona back then and she would use those skills to pull this off.

But once they'd parked, left the car and made their way to their destination, doubts began to slip into her conviction. And as she saw the looming yacht docked in the river she could feel her confidence seep away, escape into the night air and be blown away by the cool breeze.

This was not her milieu—the vessel was too enormous, too redolent of wealth as it glittered and illuminated the water of the Thames and the surrounding London landscape. But this was the world Zander inhabited and was comfortable in.

A glance sideways at him and there it was: the palpable shiver of desire. Suddenly the zing of attraction seemed stark in its utter stupidity, and a swell of panic washed over her at the enormity of the deception they had embarked upon. But it was too late now to turn and run, so somehow she'd have to tough it out.

This time tomorrow it will all be over. Think of the money.

Side by side they boarded the yacht and she braced herself, feeling the warmth of his hand on the small of her back. The heat of his touch through the thin material of her dress sent a message to her whole body, almost like a brand, as she gazed round in wonder.

The enormous wood-decked function room was bathed in light. Chandeliers and fairy lights combined to cast a magical glow of illumination. Glass-topped tables were strategically placed and suited waiters and elegant waitresses were ready to be deployed, standing next to a long table that sparkled with champagne glasses and carried silver trays of canapés.

Then the surroundings faded into irrelevance as a group of people approached them.

The Grosvenor family.

Smile. Remember your role. Play the part.

'Mum, Dad, Julia, Gemma… This is Gabby. Gabby, this is my mum, Laura, my dad, Frank, and my two sisters, Julia and Gemma.'

Gabby looked at each of them in turn, saw the appraisal in their eyes, homed in on each and every nuance. She knew she would need to read them effectively. 'It's lovely to meet you.'

Keep it cool. Talk, but not too much. Listen carefully and say what they want to hear.

All the old rules were still in play.

'And you, Gabby. We've been looking forward to it.'

Zander stepped forward. 'OK. As we discussed, there'll be plenty of time to talk later. But now it's all men and women to the pumps. I'll greet the guests as they arrive—the rest of you mingle and make sure everyone's happy. Any glitches, come and find me. Also, do your best to promote the auction items—subtly.' As they had prearranged, he glanced at Gabby. 'Will you be all right?'

'Of course, darling.'

The word was said as naturally as if she used it every day. *Damn*, she still had it. She could still play a part even if it made her nerves sizzle with anxiety. Even if this was a part that went against every particle of her character.

'You go—and if there's anything I can do to help just shout. Don't worry about me.'

A brief nod and he disappeared. Gabby took a deep breath and turned to face the Grosvenors.

'Have you had a chance to look at the auction details?' Frank asked.

She heard the kindness in his voice and knew he was trying to set her at ease. 'Yes, and I think the list is incredible.'

Items included a luxury weekend break in Portugal, a painting by a famous artist, a share in a yacht, a designer necklace from one of London's most prestigious jewellers and an afternoon driving a racing car with Alessio Bravanti himself. Each item was another reminder of the wealth of the guest list.

'I'll definitely do my best to promote it, but I think it will speak for itself.'

Now Laura smiled. 'I'm sure you'll do a great job.'

Before she could say more, a couple came

towards them with cries of greeting, and both Laura and Frank stepped forward.

'I hope we have time to talk more later, Gabby,' said Laura.

'That leaves you with us.' Julia smiled at Gabby. Her tone was friendly but her smile didn't reach her ice-blue eyes.

Gemma darted a frown at her sister and chimed in. 'Zander asked us to make sure you're OK whilst he greets the guests, and we thought we could use the time to get to know each other better, too.'

A waiter eased by, offering a tray of champagne cocktails, and Gabby took one, pretty sure that fun flings didn't ask for orange juice or a nice cup of tea at events such as this. Though she'd make sure she stuck to non-alcoholic beverages after this one—she had no intention of risking letting the mask slip.

'So…' Julia said, and Gabby tried and failed not to feel intimidated.

Julia Grosvenor would be formidable in court. Zander's eldest sister was scarily elegant, her blonde hair swept into an immaculate chignon, the ice-blue dress a vivid echo of her eye colour and a perfect showcase for her figure.

She studied Gabby with disconcerting appraisal. 'Zander tells me the two of you met recently and hit it off.'

'Yes. We were at school together, though I was in the year below him. We bumped into each other in Bath and things went from there.'

'A chance meeting?' The question was civil, but the faintest stress on the word *chance* indicated waves of scepticism.

'Come on, Jules,' Gemma interpolated. 'This isn't a courtroom and we haven't got time for a whole series of questions. Why don't we cut to the chase?'

Like Zander, Gemma was dark blonde, tall and slender, and tonight she was dressed in a deep red gown.

'We all want to know what your intentions are.'

The direct approach—Gabby welcomed it. 'I don't have any,' she said. 'We've only just started to see each other. I like Zander and he likes me, but neither of us is looking for anything serious.'

Stop there. Don't overdo it.

Both women were looking at her—two super successful, intelligent women, used to judging and evaluating people in their different fields.

Yet she had told them nothing but the slightly shaded truth.

Julia studied her for a long moment. 'If that's true, then go for it,' she said. 'Zander deserves some fun.'

Gemma smiled. 'On that note, as you have probably noticed my brother is a workaholic. Anything you can do to persuade him away from the office would be much appreciated! Now, we need to mingle...'

Soon enough they were engulfed, and Gabby's plans to embrace invisibility were scuppered by people eager to meet Zander Grosvenor's date. Panic threatened again, but Gabby combated it with a steely determination not to make a fool of herself *or* Zander. He'd trusted her to hold her own and she would play her part.

Yet her nerves twisted and tied into knots, and as the evening progressed the scenario felt more and more surreal. The pop of champagne corks, the glitter of the women's jewellery in the light of the chandeliers, the flash of expensive watches under the sleeves of designer tuxes, the conversations with their casual mention of royalty, celebrities and share portfolios made her dizzy.

To her relief, though, most people, whilst clearly curious, were also courteous—until...

Gabby sensed trouble as a red-haired woman glided towards her with a speculative, near-malicious smile on her lips.

'Hello, Gabby. I just *had* to meet you. The woman who has lured Zander Grosvenor from his monk's cell.'

Gabby tensed; she recognised the woman as a grown-up version of the playground girls who had made her life miserable as a child, with their loaded comments and taunts.

'I'm Melanie Kilton. So, tell me all about yourself—and how on earth you managed to catch Zander.'

Melanie had a smile on her lips and icicles in her blue eyes. She also had a figure to die for and a plummy voice that spoke of the fact that she'd been born to grace events like this—preferably on the arm of a man like Zander.

'I'm a librarian—' Gabby began, before realising the stupidity of her answer.

Melanie's laughter tinkled. 'How...*stereotypical*. Perhaps you and Zander will be like one of those cheesy romances where the librarian heroine falls in love with the handsome hero?'

Gabby willed her brain to come up with a witty comeback. But in the mirror of her childhood, she stood there, with the sting of humiliation behind her eyelids, willing the ground to open up and swallow her.

'I think you may be mixing up cheesy romance with classic fiction.'

Gabby turned at the sound of Zander's deep voice, half in relief, half in exasperation that she hadn't thought of the riposte herself.

'Hello, Melanie,' he continued. 'I see you haven't changed a bit.'

It seemed clear it wasn't a compliment as the redhead flushed slightly and narrowed her eyes. 'It seems that *you* have,' she said, and flicked a venomous glance at Gabby. 'And your standards have definitely dropped.'

With that she swivelled on a pointy stiletto and walked away. Gabby knew it was irrational, but the words had stung with a poison that made her insides twist.

Your standards have definitely dropped. Was everyone thinking that? Comparing her to Claudia? She knew it was petty, irrational, stupid and unnecessary to make the comparison, but she was. All those feelings of not being good enough resurfaced. But she was damned if she would let anyone see it.

'I'm sorry.' Zander's voice was level.

'What for? All you did was come to my rescue. A rescue I shouldn't have needed. You have nothing to apologise for.'

Dammit, she was snapping at him. Closing her eyes, she inhaled deeply. This wasn't Zander's fault. The issue here was that she was a fish out of water, the mutton in the flock of lambs, the woman who should never have taken the job.

'My turn to say sorry.'

'Forget it. I came to tell you the auction is going to kick off soon.'

She was sure she heard the smallest strain in his voice, so slight she wouldn't have heard it if her own sensitivities hadn't been so heightened.

'Is something wrong?' she asked. 'Was it what Melanie said about you changing?'

If the words had upset *her*, of course they must have been a hundred times more difficult for him to hear.

'This must be hard for you—everyone believing you're with another woman.'

Especially one who didn't measure up. How many people at this dazzling high-society event were whispering behind their hands, wondering why on earth Zander was with someone so ordinary?

There was a silence, and she couldn't read the expression on his face. Then, 'We need to talk.'

Hand on the small of her back again, he gently ushered her into a secluded corner, shielded from the flow of guests by an exotic arrangement of verdant green potted plants.

Zander stared down into Gabby's hazel eyes, saw the vulnerability he knew she was trying to hide, and knew Melanie's words had hurt her. He knew he couldn't let her believe he was racked with guilt because he felt he was betraying Claudia's memory.

'You're right—something *is* bothering me, but it is nothing to do with Claudia.'

Gabby's forehead creased in bemusement and question. If he prevaricated she wouldn't believe him, so he needed to tell her the truth—how hard could it be? It wouldn't kill him to admit weakness. *Much.*

'I'm nervous.'

Her eyes widened. 'Why?'

'I don't like giving speeches.'

It reminded him too much of being asked to read out loud at school—the weight of imminent humiliation as the teacher went round the class, the horrible knowledge that it would be his turn next. The fear of having to mark other people's work, his mind and body constantly geared up for fight or flight.

'As in *really* don't like it.'

As in it caused a sensation of nausea, a clamminess-inducing anxiety, a sheer funk that he loathed and had barely tamed into reluctant snarling submission.

To his relief Gabby didn't laugh; instead her expression softened.

'That sucks,' she said. 'How do you manage at work?'

'Avoidance where I can, but at work it is a little easier. I know what I'm doing and I'm the boss.' The last words were stated in a deep drawl, but she didn't smile, clearly recognising the bravado as fake.

'You know what you're doing here, as well. You know it better than anyone. What it feels like and what may help others. I know the facts and the figures—I researched those and the numbers matter—but I don't know what it feels like inside. To be that child, that young adult, that adult with dyslexia. You *do*. That's what you can bring to your audience and they will listen because you care, not because *you da boss.*'

The small smile she gave, the warmth of her voice, the sheer belief in her eyes touched him. Even if it was a touch misplaced. Because his speech focused on facts and figures; he had no intention of making it personal.

But before he could explain that she reached into her small beaded evening bag. 'You could try this, as well.'

'What's that?'

'It's a herbal remedy for anxiety—it helps calm you down. It's new, completely full of natural good things. Just a couple of drops work wonders. Really. I used it tonight and I'm sure it helps.'

'I need all the help I can get.' Taking the bottle, he took a couple of drops, handed it back.

She placed her hand on his arm. 'You hide it really well,' she said. 'I would never have imagined you were capable of even the tiniest amount of nerves and neither will anyone else.'

'It's more than a tiny amount.' The all-too-familiar flotilla of butterflies looped the loop in his gut. No amount of logic could quell them. 'I'm terrified. Bricking it. Scared. Here. Feel my heart rate.'

Taking her hand, he put it over his chest. *Bad move.* Because as she looked up at him the moment caught light, shimmered around them, and his whole being was preternaturally aware of the feather-light touch of her fingers that seemed to burn through the silk softness of his shirt. Now his heart rate ratcheted up, and this time it was nothing to do with nerves.

'Maybe *I* can help.'

Her voice was a near whisper as she stood on tiptoe and placed her other hand on his chest to steady herself before pressing her lips against his.

The lightest of butterfly kisses skimmed his lips and he closed his eyes and pulled her closer, his hands at her waist. Just as the sound of a throat being cleared caused Gabby to leap backwards so fast she nearly fell over.

Gemma grinned at him. 'Sorry to interrupt, little bro, but it's auction time.'

Zander rolled his eyes at his sister. 'We're on our way.' He waited pointedly until she'd vanished and then looked down at Gabby. 'You OK?'

'Embarrassed—but yes, I'm OK.' Her gaze met his full-on. 'Right now you need to go and knock them dead. I know you can.'

'Thank you.'

On some level alarm bells clamoured in his head—the idea that events were running away out of his control made his unease torrent. By his reckoning that was kiss number three—and, oddly, it had been more potent even than the two before.

But Gabby was right—he would consider those ramifications later. Now he had a job to do. A speech to make and an auction to run.

They made their way back to their table. Out of the corner of his eye he saw Gemma in conference with their mother, saw their quick speculative looks across at them. On the plus side, at least that kiss should have solidified the illusion that he and Gabby were in a relationship.

Hoping Gabby was correct in her analysis that not a single one of the guests would have so much as an inkling of the nervous energy that coursed through his veins, Zander went and stood on the podium, smiled and began.

He kept his speech measured, his words evenly paced as he focused on the content he had memorised and practised until he was word-perfect. He ensured his words matched the prepared presentation, carefully colour-coded so his brain could decipher and interpret the words his audience could read with ease. He went through the facts and figures, the case studies, hoping his voice was infused with the passion he felt for this subject, and then he did an audience participation exercise in which he handed out notes written in Chinese and asked people to try to read them.

As he came to an end, Gabby's voice echoed in his head.

I don't know what it feels like inside. To be that child, that young adult, that adult with dyslexia. You do. *That's what you can bring to your audience and they will listen.*

Before he knew it, unrehearsed words began to form in his brain and spill from his mouth.

'Before I wind up, I'd like to make this a little more personal. I have dyslexia myself, and I wasn't diagnosed until my late teens.'

The change in the audience was electric—a low hum that generated a charged silence. Suppressing the urge to gulp, he let the words continue.

'I know exactly what it is like to feel stupid,

to feel humiliated, to feel small and awful inside. I was lucky. I got a diagnosis and my family helped me to cope with it. A lot of children don't have that. Equally, though, if I had been diagnosed earlier, it would have made my childhood a much happier, easier place to be. I want other children out there to be given a chance. So dig deep into your wallets—because it's time for the auction!'

Gabby watched as Zander began the auction with the sale of a beautiful landscape painting—a kaleidoscope of colours that evoked the English countryside in such detail that she almost felt she could step into it. But she realised it was *his* pitch that called attention to and emphasised the merit of the artist, made her want to buy the picture, made her appreciate every stroke the artist had touched to the canvas.

He talked, caused laughter and a friendly competitive spirit, encouraged people to bid without being aggressive—it was a masterly performance, made all the more admirable by the speech he had made earlier.

Gabby hugged the knowledge to herself that she and only she knew what it had cost him, the emotions he'd had to master. She realised that she was proud of him.

Whoa. Careful, Gabs.

But right now she didn't want to be careful—and there was nothing wrong with admiration anyway. There were numerous people she admired. Winston Churchill, Mother Teresa, her grandparents... Problem was, she didn't think she'd be studying the way Winston's hair curled on the nape of his neck, or the lithe grace with which he moved. Whereas as she looked at Zander, her tummy was tied in knots of desire.

Next to her, Julia cleared her throat, and Gabby could only pray she hadn't been drooling.

'He's doing a pretty good job, isn't he?'

Turning, Gabby attempted what she hoped was a casual smile. 'Definitely. You have to admire that passion in someone—I think Winston Churchill was the same.'

Had she really said that?

Julia looked slightly puzzled, clearly wondering the same thing, and Gabby hurried on. 'Anyway, it's fantastic to see people having fun and bidding so much.'

As she spoke, the gavel pounded to indicate

the painting had gone for an exorbitant sum and Zander moved on.

'Next up is an incredible trip to the sunny climes of Portugal. A romantic three-night trip in…'

Julia nodded. 'I'm not sure if Zander told you, but the reason he decided to do this event wasn't only because of his own dyslexia. It's because my son, Freddy, was diagnosed with it recently, and that seemed to trigger Zander into an absolute determination to do something. He said he wants to show Freddy it's nothing to be ashamed of.'

Great! Something else to admire about the man. Just what Gabby needed. But it was impossible not to appreciate the gesture, the drive to do more than simply offer personal support.

'Freddy's lucky, really—early diagnosis makes an enormous difference. I don't think Mum will ever forgive herself for not working it out sooner with Zander. You see, Gemma and I were high achievers academically and she expected Zander to be the same. To be honest, she was baffled when he wasn't. Never unkind, but her pep talks and lectures and the muted disappointment must have been hard for him. Of course, he's achieved a lot now!'

'Yes. And Zander certainly doesn't seem to blame anyone.'

'We feel guilty all the same. I used to tease him sometimes. Now, when I look at my Freddy and imagine people teasing him, it makes me so mad I could spit.'

Before Gabby could respond, a cheer went up and they looked to the podium as Laura Grosvenor stepped up on to the stage.

'Oh. Mum's won the holiday! She must have got it for her and Dad's anniversary.' Julia smiled fondly at her parents. 'Dad is really quiet, but I don't know what Mum would do without him. He is her rock. I'll just go and congratulate them...'

The rest of the auction items went for equally exorbitant sums, and the gavel pounded a final time to much applause. But before Zander could step down, Laura Grosvenor climbed on to the stage again and took the microphone.

'Sorry, everyone. One last thing. Zander—I am very proud of all you have achieved, tonight and throughout your life. And it occurs to me that you deserve a holiday. So here you go—this is for you. A three-day break to Portugal. And I'm sure we *all* know who you'll be taking!'

As the whole room turned to look at her, Gabby strove to fix a smile of surprise and delight on her lips, even as her brain churned in incoherent panic.

CHAPTER SEVEN

SOMEHOW GABBY REMAINED in role, smile in place, as she watched the scene play itself out on the podium. After a split second of shock, Zander thanked his mother with apparent sincere appreciation, cracked a couple of jokes with an aplomb she could only envy, and then he and his mother descended from the stage.

Stay in role.

Horribly conscious of all the eyes on her, she rose and walked towards Laura, hand outstretched.

'Thank you *so* much. That is amazingly kind of you—though you really shouldn't have included me.'

Laura's gaze went from one to the other of them. 'Why ever not? I've had a look at the conditions and you can go as early as next week if you like.'

Her blue gaze was disconcertingly perceptive—but, charade or no charade, Gabby knew

she had to try to wriggle out of this somehow.
She might not have been listening completely to
the description, but words like *sun-kissed*, *romantic*, *cosy* and *perfect for two* lingered in her
memory.

'I feel a little guilty accepting such a generous
gift. I mean, you hardly know me.'

'Yes, but I *do* know Zander. And I know he
hasn't had a holiday in five years.' The implication hovered in the air. *Since Claudia.* 'All
he has done is work. So I would love for him to
have some downtime, and now seems like the
perfect opportunity.' Laura glanced from one
face to the other. 'I'm counting on you, Gabby,
to convince Zander that all work and no play is
not a good thing!'

'I'll try,' Gabby said and wondered if her nose
was having a Pinocchio moment. 'But if I can't,
then you must promise me that you will accept
the holiday back for you and your husband.'

'We came back from a cruise just recently.'

'And *we* don't want it.' Gemma and Julia had
materialised.

Gemma continued, 'I've got a wedding to plan
and my honeymoon is already booked.'

'I have work commitments, no one to go with

and the kids to think of,' Julia pointed out. 'So it's all yours.'

Any more protest would only fuel the suspicion that was already on the verge of sparking, so Gabby tucked her hand into Zander's arm. 'Then all I can do is thank you.'

'You're very welcome.'

The rest of the evening passed in a blur. Zander's proximity as they sat through dinner was both a solace and a menace. Not even the food— marinated salmon, truffle potatoes, a fillet of beef so rare and tender it made sense of the melt-in-the-mouth cliché—could completely distract from her body's reaction to his proximity or the sense of impending doom that the idea of Portugal had brought on.

But Gabby did her best to focus on the job at hand, striving to consolidate the illusion of a relationship and to make the event a success. She told herself that, between them, she and Zander would work out a way to mitigate or better yet wipe out the Portugal disaster.

Finally the last guest departed, the last goodbye was said and only the family were left.

Julia stepped forward and gave Zander a hug. 'Well done, little bro. This was a fabulous event and thank you for doing it. I'll show Freddy the pictures.'

'You do that—and tell him I'll be round soon.'

Turning to Gabby with a smile that made her seem way less scary, Julia added, 'Gabby, it was great to meet you—and if I don't see you before, I'll see you at the wedding. Have a fabulous time in Portugal.'

Gabby smiled, watching the remaining fare-wells and witnessing the sheer warmth and affection that existed in the Grosvenor family. A part of her felt a yearning for that sort of family closeness. Lord knew she loved her grandmother, but Lucille was all she had. And that meant one day, in the scheme of things, she would be alone. The thought cloaked her in sadness.

Goodbyes finally finished, they made their way to the car. Gabby waited until they were inside, seat belts secured, before she spoke. 'What are we going to do?'

'Drive back to my apartment?'

'I meant about Portugal.'

'I know. I suggest we both try to figure out a strategy and we can talk about it when we get back. But first—thank you for everything you did tonight. You played your part to perfection, but you also did a fantastic job of talking to people about dyslexia. That wasn't part of the deal and I appreciate it.'

'I wanted to help. It's not a topic I've really thought about very much until recently, but the research I did showed me how important a topic it is. And you did, too.'

'I really do believe the more people discuss it and raise awareness the better. So thank you.'

He turned to flash her a quick smile and her tummy flip-flopped, tiredness suddenly forgotten as awareness simmered. And this was in a *car*—what would happen on a romantic beach getaway?

Determinedly closing her eyes, she leant her head back and tried to think of a strategy, a way out. But her brain refused to cooperate; instead, images drifted through her mind of herself and Zander on a beach, sitting on the sand, his fingers massaging sun cream into her back...

'Gabby? We're here.'

Sitting upright, she opened her eyes, blinked fiercely to dispel the lingering stupid fantasy and opened the car door.

They walked through the lobby, into the lift and out again, then into the apartment, and this time she followed him into an enormous living area.

More neutrality here, mixed with a minimalist feel that didn't look like a design choice. It looked like the result of utter disinterest. Two large leather sofas, two chairs, a flat-screen television. A coffee table. More empty walls. No pictures, no photographs, no clutter, no cushions. Bland mixed with impersonal.

It was enough to temporarily distract her from the urgency of the Portugal fiasco and prompt a question. 'Did you only move in recently?'

He looked puzzled as he glanced around the room, as if seeing it through her eyes. 'A couple of years ago. Once I was sure that the business was secure, I figured it made more sense to own than to rent. Alessio persuaded me that a penthouse apartment was what I needed, and it seemed like a good enough investment.'

As he spoke, he tugged off his tie and unbuttoned the top button of his shirt with an exhalation of relief. Gabby's gaze fell on the small triangle of exposed skin and her breath caught in her throat. Her fingers itched with an insane desire to step forward and unbutton the next button, and the next. A reaction presumably brought on by panic and tiredness and his sheer proximity.

'Did you choose the furniture?' It was the best small talk she could conjure up as her gaze focused on his hands, studied the strength of his fingers, the broad wrists, the way he pushed his shirtsleeves up to reveal his muscled forearms.

'Yes.' He frowned. 'I just ordered online. I seem to spend more time in the office or travelling on business anyway, so this is more than enough for my needs. It's just a place to eat and sleep, really.' As if sensing her bemusement, he folded his arms in an almost defensive position. 'I take it you disagree?'

'It's not that I disagree—it's more that I don't get it. My flat is where I eat and sleep, but I think of it as more than that. It's my *home*.' Her sanctuary. She utterly loved the security, the familiarity, the fact that it existed, was there every day. 'I have a lovely landlord who has let me decorate and paint how I want to. I scoured the markets and charity shops in Bath and I've picked up and restored some gorgeous furniture.'

'So you rent?'

'Yes.'

If she wanted, she could buy rather than rent, but the deposit needed would take all her savings—which were earmarked for care for Lucille. Plus a certain amount of her salary went each month on providing a home help for her gran. But that wasn't something she wanted to discuss with Zander.

She sat down on the armchair, which despite its *meh*-ness was at least comfortable. 'Anyway, we have more important things to discuss. What are we going to do? About Portugal?'

He walked over to a drinks cabinet in the corner of the room. 'Drink?' The suggestion was accompanied by a rueful smile that, despite the situation, made her tummy dip.

'Ha ha!'

'Obviously I am not suggesting drink as an answer to the problem, but I think it may help deaden the pain of my answer. I can offer you whisky or wine.'

'Red wine would be lovely.'

Minutes later he handed her a glass and then sat opposite her. 'We'll have to go.'

'Go?' Her voice reached an octave she'd hitherto thought impossible, and she sipped the rich ruby wine as a palliative.

'Yes.'

To her irrational chagrin, his voice held no enthusiasm. But it did hold conviction.

'Unless you have an idea that would get us out of it without hurting my mother's feelings and unmasking us as impostors.'

'Can't you have a work emergency?'

'Not on a permanent basis.'

'But if we do go...'

Her voice trailed off. If they did go, *what*? They'd end up in bed together? That was ridiculous—she was a grown woman, not an adolescent. Yes, she was attracted to Zander, but surely she could get through three days without actually jumping him?

'Won't it be awkward?'

'It doesn't have to be awkward. Yes, it is meant to be a romantic break, but there won't be anyone watching us. We can spend our time however we like. I was planning on a working weekend, but I can work from anywhere.'

Hurt pinged, along with a sudden sense of outrage that he could be so unaffected, could imagine sitting there and working rather than spending time with her.

But you know he's right.

After all, every time they spent any amount of time in close proximity they ended up in a clinch. Plus, this was a fake romance—so why would he *want* to spend time with her?

Another sip of wine and she studied his expression, wondering if there was just a hint of a clench to his jawline as she told herself that his solution was the correct one. Go to Portugal and spend their time separately. And yet...

'I don't think a working weekend will work. Your family will ask questions when we get back...expect some photographs of us together. Julia strikes me as a woman who likes evidence. More to the point, your mum gave you this holiday in good faith. She wants you to have a break. Surely you owe her at least a credible pretence that you've done that?'

Colour touched his cheekbones and then he nodded. 'You're right. I should have thought of that.' Now his expression was rueful. 'I guess I'm so used to working weekends I've forgotten how to even *fake* a break.' He reached forward and picked up the brochure and the details about the trip. 'I guess we will have to spend some time together after all.'

Well done, Gabby. She'd now persuaded him

to spend time with her. A little voice questioned her motives—maybe that was what she actually wanted?

Holding out her hand, she forced her expression to remain cool. 'If you like, I'll do a bit of research...figure out the best things to do.' That way at least she could retain some semblance of control.

'Sure. That would be good.'

Taking care not to so much as brush against his fingers, she took the folder and rose to her feet. 'Now that's settled, if it's OK with you, I'll hit your spare room. I'll be out of your hair first thing tomorrow morning.'

Literally—her plan was to sneak out at daybreak.

'Then, next stop—Portugal.'

A week later, Zander glanced across at Gabby as she clicked her seat belt on and settled back in the luxurious first-class seat. Simply dressed in cropped linen trousers and a blue-and-cream-striped T-shirt, she looked utterly gorgeous.

Over the past days he'd immersed himself in work, taken some time out to spend with his niece and nephew, caught a beer with Alessio—

but Gabby had popped into his head with a persistent, disconcerting frequency.

Logic told him that it was all to do with physical attraction, and further informed him that, however mutual the attraction, it would be a bad idea to succumb.

Instinct warned that it would bring complications of the type he didn't want. Gabby had made it more than clear that a short-term relationship was not what she wanted. She wanted a relationship like her grandparents had had. He respected that, but he knew he couldn't offer it. So the best way forward was to keep a lid on the attraction.

He opened his netbook and settled down to work—yet he couldn't resist the occasional glimpse out of the corner of his eye. The gloss of her chestnut hair, the length of her long slim legs, the small frown of concentration that creased her forehead as she read her book…

The two-hour flight was achieved in near silence, broken only by polite banalities over the quality of the food. Gabby had clearly decided the best way to get through their 'romantic break' was the use of platitudes to combat the danger of proximity. It seemed as good a strategy as any.

'Nice airport,' he said as they alighted from the aircraft.

'I don't have a lot of airport experience, but I'm sure you know what you're talking about.'

Their discussion on airports and Tarmac was sustained through customs and baggage control and then segued seamlessly into comments on the hire car.

Once they were en route to Sintra, he sensed Gabby relax, as if now his focus was on driving and navigation she could afford to drop her guard and enjoy the scenery and the heat of the Portuguese sunshine as they made their way to their destination.

And what a destination it was.

Gabby gave a small gasp as they arrived. 'This is...*amazing*. I knew Sintra was in a natural park, with beautiful scenery, but I didn't realise it would be like this.'

Neither had he. Hills covered in lush forest contrasted with a rugged coastline. Verdant greens, azure blues, rich browns all combined in a kaleidoscopic panorama of vibrant colour.

'The villa is on the outskirts of Sintra, so thankfully we don't have to drive through town.

The owner recommended walking and using public transport.'

But despite the factual nature of his words, Zander could feel himself relax, too, almost against his will. The scent of eucalyptus and the inexplicable sense of time slowed down pervaded the very air in the car, and for a moment he almost wished this was a real break, a real holiday. That he and Gabby were a real...

He wrenched his thoughts from the impossible and focused on navigating the narrow winding country road that led to the villa.

'Holy moly...' Gabby whispered as they climbed out of the car. Her hazel eyes were wide with wonder, her lips slightly parted. 'It's... fantastical, phantasmal—I mean, I can't believe it's real.'

It truly was idyllic. Whitewashed stone walls, a low roof, a doorway trailing with plants, wooden framed windows that gleamed pristinely, a mosaic patio garden. The scent of pine, the drone of bees, sun-dappled greenery. The villa could have been lifted from a book of fairy tales.

'And look!'

Her hand landed on Zander's bare forearm and the touch sent an instant ripple of sensation over his skin, a tantalising hint of a promise that he knew couldn't be kept.

The expression on her face was so alight with enthusiasm and awe that he found it hard to take his eyes from her and follow the direction of her gaze. But he did, taking in the magnificence of the view, the steep descent of the valley, the shine of the sea in the late-morning sunshine, the medieval walls of the Moorish castle that over-looked the town.

'Breathtaking.'

Yet even now he wasn't sure if it was Gabby or the scene before him that had caused his lungs to constrict, and he turned back to the villa.

'Shall we make sure it's solid and look inside?'

Gabby nodded and together they approached the aquamarine front door, where he halted, leant down and retrieved a key from under a flower-pot.

'The owner should have left full instructions and some provisions inside.' Turning the key, he pushed the door open and they stepped inside.

The stone walls were unpainted, a higgledy-piggledy pattern of shades of cream and brown and grey. The living area was small but comfort-ably furnished, with a white love seat scattered with scarlet cushions and two plump armchairs in cool cream. There was a small kitchen area in the background, with a display cabinet holding an array of brightly patterned plates, cheerful curtains at the window. Tucked away was the bathroom—a small room cleverly designed to include a marble sink and a state-of-the-art shower. A winding staircase led the way up to a mezzanine level under the gables where a double bed sat.

'You can have the bed,' he said. 'I can easily manage down here.'

'How?' They both scanned the size of the sofa. 'There is no way you'll fit on that.'

'Yes, but neither will you.'

'Then we'll take turns,' she said firmly.

'Well, you have upstairs tonight and then we'll see.'

He followed her up the winding wooden stairs, lined with bright red iron banisters wrought in thin wavy lines. Once on the mezzanine, they stood in silence. The entire area was dominated by the double bed, which had an ornate curved headboard and was tucked snugly under eaves and gables.

Turning away from it, she said, 'What a beautiful bed.' Instantly heat touched her face. 'That is *not* what I meant. I meant to say view. What a beautiful *view*.'

'It is.' He couldn't help it. He kept his gaze focused on her face and her blush deepened.

'Out there,' she said, and he followed the pointing of her finger.

Gabby was right. The window framed a burst of flowers, a kaleidoscope of colours and scents that wafted inside. Yet right now he'd prefer to look at Gabby. *Not good.*

He headed for the stairs.

Once downstairs, Gabby sat on one of the armchairs. 'Right. As discussed, I did some research and...' She paused. 'What?'

He realised that without meaning to he had started grinning. '"I'll do a bit of research." It's the Gabby Johnson catchphrase.'

'Go figure.' But she was smiling, too. 'I *like* research. I like to have a plan. And, honestly, I enjoyed it. Sintra is an incredible place—there's so much to do. A palace, a medieval castle, and it all looks so very magical. I wish—' She broke off and regrouped. 'I've basically come up with a few things we can do, take some photos and garner enough information so that we can make sure your family believe we had a proper romantic break. *And* you will still have time to work.'

'Perfect. I'll make coffee, then we can figure out what to do next.'

CHAPTER EIGHT

AS HE SCOOPED coffee into the cafetière, Zander pushed down a sudden, inexplicable, *ridiculous* sense of regret. There was nothing *to* regret— this was an enforced break and he needed to work. Yet Gabby's enthusiasm, her sense of the magical, had infused him with an unmistakable tint of dissatisfaction at the prospect of work, and with an urge to explore Sintra and see it through Gabby's eyes. *Daft.* He'd never been one for beach holidays or romantic breaks and now was definitively not the time to start.

With a shake of his head he poured the coffee and returned to the lounge area, where Gabby sat on the sofa, laptop resting on her knees.

'OK. So what's the plan?' Handing her a mug, he sat down in the other armchair.

'Well, there is so much that we can do it's been quite hard to narrow it down. This place is like a tourist treasure trove—fairy-tale castles, beaches, fishing villages...'

As he watched her, something tugged in his chest. Her enthusiasm, the way she described the places, was still doing something strange to him.

'You choose—I'm good with any of them.'

'Nope. It's important *you* choose.' Her face was serious now. 'The whole point of this charade is to make your family happy, so we need to do this properly. What would you *like* to do? Apart from work.'

It occurred to him that he had no idea. 'I really don't mind.'

She frowned, hesitated. 'What sort of holidays did you and Claudia go on?'

'We mostly holidayed with her parents. They'd bought an old chateau out in France and we spent the holidays helping them renovate it.' He hadn't enjoyed those holidays—he'd known Claudia's parents didn't really approve of him, though he'd never been sure as to why. Perhaps they had seen something he hadn't been able to—had known that in reality he and Claudia weren't suited.

'So even that was a sort of working holiday?' Gabby asked. 'What about family holidays when you were young?'

'We used to go down to Cornwall and Devon and camp mostly. Money was tight, but we still had a wonderful time. I spent loads of time swimming in the sea and trying to make surfboards out of driftwood.'

It was a long time since he had thought back to those holidays, those hours of happiness away from school, away from the scent of failure and humiliation. Free to be himself, free to swim and run and think and plan how one day, somehow, he would prove to the world that he wasn't stupid.

'Then I have the perfect thing for you to do. You can go surfing! Why not have a lesson? On a real surfboard?'

For a moment he was tempted, but then he shook his head. 'No point. I haven't the time or the inclination to take it up as a hobby, so why bother?'

'Because it might be *fun*! No one is going to demand a commitment from you to take it up as a lifestyle. Plus, if you enjoy it, why *not* take it up as a hobby? You surely can't work all the time, every weekend.'

'Surfing sounds like a time-consuming hobby and I don't have the time.' Right or wrong, his entire focus was on his business and that was the way he liked it.

'OK. But one afternoon surfing won't impact your company, will it?'

Put like that, he realised how absurd he sounded, and wondered at his own reluctance to kick back and enjoy something other than work. 'Of course not.'

'Good. Then that's decided. I'll call them and book you in.'

'What about you?'

'Uh-uh.' She shook her head. 'No way. Not my thing at all. I wish it was—I mean, the idea of mastering the waves is obviously incredible—but I can't imagine doing it. I wish I was that sort of person but I'm not. I'll sit on the sand and watch.'

He frowned. When he'd first met her hadn't she said the same?

I wish I was the sort of woman who would jump at this, but I'm not.

'How do you know? Have you tried it before?'

'No. I don't need to. The whole idea leaves me cold—or rather shaking with terror.'

'Can you swim?'

'Yes. In a pool I'm pretty competent, but the thought of swimming in the sea doesn't appeal. Too scary.'

'But you might be a natural—you might love it.'

'Or I might drown.'

'Unlikely on a summer day, on a safe beach with an instructor *and* me there. I think you should give it a try.'

'Well, I appreciate your thought, but I don't want to.'

'But if you try it and find it too frightening, you can always stop.' Perhaps *he* should stop, but he sensed that deep down she did want to do this.

'I'm already finding it too frightening and I'm on dry land, miles away from the sea.'

'But—'

'Stop with the *buts*. The idea of falling in, of the waves sucking me in, pulling me away, of drowning, of choking, not being able to breathe, not coming back... *That* is too frightening.'

Her knuckles had tightened white against the brown enamel of the coffee mug and he reached out and gently took it from her clasp.

'Back off, OK?'

'OK. I'm sorry. I didn't realise it was such a deep-rooted fear.'

'And I'm sorry. I didn't mean to snap.' She closed her eyes and inhaled deeply, then re-opened them. 'It's OK. To be honest, I hadn't realised myself how much it would still affect me. It's silly, really. I just have a vividly overactive imagination. My grandfather loved swimming in the sea. Really loved it. But it terrified me. We'd often go to the coast on weekends and I'd watch him go out further and further, getting smaller and smaller, and I'd get more and more scared. Because I realised that the sea didn't understand or care that he was one of only two people I had in the world to look after me. I would imagine the sea as the enemy, luring him away from me, away from the shore until he wouldn't be able to get back.'

Her arms wrapped defensively over her stomach, as if she could feel the same twist of hollow dread now.

The image hit his brain with shocking clarity. A young Gabby sitting on a beach, watching, dreading, hoping... And, given the loss of her parents, her fear would have had a horrible validity—her reliance on her grandparents must have been absolute.

'But he came back,' he said gently.

'Yes, he did. Every time. It should have made the anxiety lessen, but it didn't. Each time I figured the probability had increased that *this* time would be the one when it all went tragic. I'd make so many bargains in my head. If he comes back, I'll give up chocolate…make straight As… I never told him how scared I was because I knew how much he loved swimming in the sea and I didn't want to spoil it for him.' She reached for her cup. 'I'd changed his life enough.'

The last words had been said so softly he suspected she wasn't even aware she'd spoken the thought aloud.

'Anyway—lesson learnt. The sea is not for me.'

'Maybe.' Zander leant forward. 'But perhaps your fear was that you would lose your grandfather, not a fear of the sea *per se*.'

'Perhaps. But the bottom line is I can live without surfing quite happily. My life won't be blighted if I don't book myself in for a lesson.'

'I understand that, but your life might well be enhanced if you *do*.'

'Why does this matter to you?'

'Because fear is debilitating. I spent my whole childhood afraid that I was stupid, scared of books and of being found out. For years I devised strategies so that people would think I could read. If I hadn't been so scared I think I would have asked for help. If there is one thing

I've learnt it's that I don't like being scared and that fear can change you. Facing fear can change your life. I'm not saying surfing will change your life, but in some ways not being afraid of the sea will make your life better.'

'How?'

'Let's say you've met Mr Right and one day you're on the beach with him and your two kids. Do you want to pass your fear on, or do you want to swim with your family in the sea?'

Gabby narrowed her eyes. 'No fair.'

'The end justifies the means. Come on, Gabby. Book us both a surfing lesson for later today. Then let's go down to the beach and have a go at swimming in the sea.'

'Now?'

'Yup. There's no time like the present.'

Panic widened her eyes and she shook her head. 'Hang on. If I have to move out of my comfort zone, so do you.'

'OK. Name it. What do you want me to do?' Even as he spoke the words he had a vague inkling of their stupidity.

'You take a *real* holiday. No more work.'

The tables had turned so fast he hadn't seen the edges coming for him. 'I can't do that.'

'Why not? Would your whole business collapse if you took a break?'

Again, put like that it sounded absurd, and yet the idea of no work... It *scared* him.

Her lips tipped in the tiniest of smirks. 'If the idea scares you, you should face up to that fear. Or we can give up on the whole idea. You work—I stay clear of the sea. Deal?'

Zander hesitated. Work kept him sane, gave him purpose, satisfied his need for success. It was his drive. But it was nuts that the idea of a break *scared* him. Time to put his money where his mouth was and face the fear down.

'No. No way. I'll take a break and you'll swim in the sea and *then* we are going to surf. Deal?'

Silence and then she nodded. 'Deal.'

'And...' Whilst he was at it he would face down the fear of spending time with Gabby, too—the fear that he couldn't control the attraction factor. 'If I'm taking a break, then maybe we could spend some time together. As friends.'

'Friends?'

He could hear the doubt, and an echoing inner voice questioned the sanity of the suggestion. It appeared that he was launching from stupidity to stupidity in an ever-increasing circle.

'Yes, friends. Why not? We both accept that physical attraction exists and can't be acted on, but that doesn't mean we have to be afraid of it. We should face it down.'

'Combat it with friendship? I guess it's worth a try...'

'Friends it is.' He held out his hand. 'Deal?'

'Deal,' she echoed and placed her hand in his.

The simple touch called the whole pact into question, causing a temptation to hold on, to circle his thumb round the tender pad of her palm. Instead he shook it and dropped it.

'I'll call the office.'

'I'll call the surf school.'

Gabby tried and failed to subdue the odd buzz of anticipation that laced her veins as they left the house and headed for Sintra and the tram station. True, there was a knot of anxiety in the pit of her tummy at the thought of the forthcoming swim, sea and surf experience, but her nerves were overlaid by the reassurance offered in the sheer bulk of Zander at her side. Perhaps they were also helped by the drops of herbal remedy she'd hastily taken whilst changing.

The idea of the next few days caused a fizz

inside her she knew she should subdue. *Three days with Mr Wrong—remember, Gabby?* But the reminder did nothing to dispel the bubble of happiness. And why not? It was OK to enjoy the company of a friend. And friendship was a *good* thing. Plus, maybe getting to know each other better would help dilute their physical attraction.

Inside her that little voice of reality dissolved into hysterical laughter. *Yeah, right,* it jeered, but Gabby refused to acknowledge it. This would work.

And so she revelled in the sunshine as it soaked her skin, and in the feel of the streets under her sandals—as if she could absorb the historic beauty of Sintra through its cobbles.

Central to the town, the Gothic National Palace was a monument to history, with its whitewashed rambling walls and the iconic coned chimneys that reached for the unending blue of the sky.

'Apparently Hans Christian Andersen said they looked like champagne bottles,' she told Zander, suddenly happy that she could talk to him as if to a friend, no longer using the words as small talk.

He glanced down at her and suddenly he smiled—a smile that scorched her and sent all thoughts of friendship rushing into the shadows.

'More research?' he asked.

'Absolutely. The history of the palace is fascinating. I've always loved history. I nearly did it at uni.'

'What stopped you?'

'Not vocational enough. I wasn't really sure what I would do with a history degree—and I really didn't want to come out of university with a massive student loan.' Gabby had always known that her priority was her grandparents—ensuring she could care for them. 'So I decided to skip uni—go a different route. I worked in a library and studied for a diploma in librarianship at the same time, and luckily I love it. And I get to keep history as a hobby.'

'So tell me about the palace.'

She frowned. 'Why?'

'Because I'm interested and because I like the way your face lights up when you talk about things that interest you.'

They were words a friend might use, but it didn't feel like that. His eyes held warmth and his gaze caressed her skin.

'OK. Um…' For a moment all her research deserted her, but then finally memory kicked in. 'The palace was built on the site of a Moorish fortress way back in medieval times, and Portuguese royals used it as their home. Some of them were born and died here. One of the best stories about it is that in 1582 four ambassadors from Japan visited Europe and came to Sintra—how brilliant is that? Wherever they went they were treated with respect; they were seen as a living letter from Japan. I think that's wonderful—that centuries ago people showed respect to other cultures...cultures that must have been so different.'

Gabby came to a stop, aware that her voice had quickened into a torrent of words.

'Sorry. Too much information.'

'Nope. I'm genuinely interested.'

And still his gaze rested on her with a glint that quickened her pulse.

'The tram station is this way.'

They walked onwards, and, as luck would have it, within minutes of their arrival a bright-coloured, old-fashioned tram trundled in. They joined the throng of people and squashed on to a wooden seat, but it was no matter that the carriage was crowded. In fact her body almost whooped at the chance to be legitimately pressed up close to Zander, to breathe in his scent, to feel his hard, muscular thigh against hers as they undertook the slow, noisy journey from town to coastline.

Three-quarters of an hour later they alighted at the beach, and suddenly she began to question the wisdom of her decision. A glance at the sea with its calm majesty should have reassured her, but somehow its vast expanse triggered anxiety and her footsteps slowed, her tummy churned.

And there was another issue to contend with. Like it or not, she had to take off her blue-and-white floral summer dress and reveal the swimsuit underneath. A completely serviceable plain black swimsuit, chosen for its simplicity. Yet self-consciousness engulfed her as she pulled out the changing towel from her bag and began some complicated manoeuvring.

Zander observed her for a moment and then, without a shred of embarrassment, tugged his T-shirt over his head, leaving him standing on the sand patiently in his board shorts.

A deep breath and her dress dropped in a silky puddle to the sand, leaving her with the towel still covering her. *Right.* She wriggled out of it with as much nonchalance as possible, feeling the heat of the sun's rays warm her skin, trying not to feel exposed as she stared at the waves.

He held out his hand. 'Let's paddle to start.'

A moment of hesitation and then she placed her hand in his, told herself that friends held hands, that it was a gesture of reassurance. Nothing more.

Yet as they walked towards the gently lapping waves it *felt* like more. Skin against skin was a safe anchor, for sure, but it held an added overtone of awareness, made more acute by her sideways glimpses at his muscular chest, the smooth sculpture of his shoulders, and heightened by the fear of the water ahead of her and the crunch of the sand underfoot as each step took her closer.

Then cool waves washed over her feet, snaked around her calves, and she halted.

'Standing here, all my fears seem groundless,' she said. 'The sea seems so innocent. But when I look out there I remember that in fact all I have to do is go out of my depth and I could drown.' She shrugged. 'I guess it's a pretty apt life analogy, isn't it?'

'No. Because it is possible to go out of your depth and *not* drown. Some people swim the Channel. Or you can go by boat.'

'At greater risk. It's safer to stick to paddling.'

'But then you never get to leave the shore.'

Sensing that there was something more in his words, something deeper than the superficial, she turned to him, studied his expression. 'Some people are happy on the shore.'

'Yes. They are.'

Now his eyes were definitely clouded, and the words held an unhappiness that was palpable—almost a self-reproach that she didn't understand.

'Are you?' he asked.

'I...' She looked out to sea, unsure how to answer. There were so many times when she yearned to be a different person, someone willing to take risks, someone braver, more extroverted, more... Just *more*. But she was who she was. 'Of course,' she said. 'And there is nothing wrong with that.'

'No,' he agreed quietly. 'There isn't. If you don't want to swim in the sea you don't have to. You've kept your part of the bargain. You're here. In the water.' Zander ran a hand over his face. 'You don't have to do this,' he said. 'I shouldn't have made you, and if you don't feel comfortable, then don't do it.'

His tone of voice was so at odds with the Zander of earlier that it jolted her out of her funk and she turned to face him, studying his face and noting the shadow that crossed his eyes.

It was he who now faced the waves, his body shifting away from hers. 'I have a bad habit of bulldozing people into doing what suits *me*. And I have no right to do that.'

'You didn't bulldoze me. I agreed to do this. But there's no point fibbing. I *am* terrified.'

Gabby caught her bottom lip between her teeth and glared at the sea, wishing she could will it into submission. Life didn't work like that, though. Zander hadn't been able to will his dyslexia into submission—he'd had to face the fear and work at it, learn to live with it.

Now she had a choice to make: she could take the easy option—turn away from this, tell herself there was no need to swim in the sea. Or she could try. She could swim away from the shore. And come back.

'I am going to try. Show me. You swim out. But not too far.'

'Sure.'

There was no hesitation, not even a sliver of the anxiety that instantly consumed her as he strode forward into the water, increasing his pace. And then he was swimming with strong, sure strokes, cleaving through the water until he flipped over on to his back, then floating for a moment and treading water to face her and wave.

The panic began to swirl. That urge to call him back rose, and she swallowed it down. The sea was calm. There were no rip tides or currents; they had checked. It was safe. But she wanted him to come back.

As if he knew that Zander reversed course, and minutes later he was beside her again. Water dripped from his dark blonde hair, glinted in the sunlight. His features were relaxed; he looked younger, happier…exhilarated. *Gorgeous.* A man who didn't live on the metaphorical shore.

'Right. What's the best way to do this?' she asked.

'First you need to remember that you can swim—of course it's different than a pool, but it's still water. You do have the ability to navigate the sea as long as you respect it. Respect is healthy. Also, remember we've done all the safety checks on tides and currents. Next, you need to get used to the temperature—come in a little further, get a feel for it.'

His calm deep tones helped and Gabby nodded, stepped forward, felt the resistance of the water against her legs. She was relieved that the water, though cold, was already sun warmed in the late afternoon as she tried to absorb and define the swirl of the current.

'Watch your breathing,' Zander said. 'It's easy when you're a bit anxious and in water to breathe shallowly. Better to focus on deeper breaths— inhale and feel your diaphragm move.'

Now it wasn't only his voice but his presence that helped. She walked a little further, feeling the sand rougher now between her toes, and she looked down, wondered what lurked in the swirling turquoise depths.

'It's OK. Let's just swim out a little way—a few strokes, slowly and methodically. Then we'll flip over on to our backs and you can look at the sky and float. Does that sound OK? I'll be right next to you.'

She made the first few strokes and then fear, unfamiliarity and the idea of the unknown segued into panic. Even the ability to swim, to breathe seemed to desert her. Then came his voice.

'Now on to your back. It's fine, Gabby.'

On automatic, she managed to turn over, her

panic assuaged by the feel of his hands under her, offering support, and she concentrated on breathing and floating. Then he released her and she gazed up at the still, intense blue of the sky, open and vast and oddly calming. She was doing it—actually being carried by the waves—and disbelief fought with sheer exhilaration.

'You're doing great. You ready to head back to shore? Or do you want to go a little further?'

One last look at the sky and Gabby switched to treading water. She looked at the shore—the sandy curve was still not too far away—and turned her head to look out at the sea. There were other swimmers out further...a few surfers along the waves.

'Let's go a little further. I'd like to actually swim.'

'How about twenty-five strokes and then we'll turn and head back? Make sure you breathe on both sides if you're doing front crawl—and maybe swap to breaststroke if you feel panicked. That way you can see where you're going better.'

Again Zander struck the right tone—acceptance without question, an assumption that she could do it alongside common sense and practical advice. That and the knowledge that he'd be there right beside her enabled Gabby to turn away from the shore and strike out, counting the strokes in her head, keeping time, feeling the cleave of the water against her limbs.

She reached twenty-five and stopped, turned and looked back at the shore, now peopled by what looked like the equivalent of toy figures. She could feel the rise of panic; the growing idea that she wouldn't make it back. She saw an image of Lucille, left all alone, Gabby's promise to her grandfather to look after her broken by a stupid urge to try to be different, to change her personality.

Suddenly the limbs that had felt so strong, so buoyant just seconds before trembled, her lungs refused to cooperate, and an urgent need for oxygen caused her ears to pound.

'Gabby. It's fine. You're doing fine. Twenty-five more strokes and you'll be back in touching distance of the shore. You *will* make it back.'

She opened eyes she hadn't even known she'd closed and looked at Zander's expression. He was serious, his belief in his own words so strong she could swear they formed an aura. Every fibre of her being wanted to ask him to tow her back, and she knew he would do so without question or censure. But something deeper told her that was the easy option and one she would regret taking.

'Let's go.'

This time it was harder, each stroke more of an effort, but eventually she hit twenty-five, surfaced—and saw the shoreline! A few more strokes and she could stand. Her questing toes found and crunched on the seabed and she waded towards the shore, reached it, turned and looked back out to sea.

'I did it! I swam out and I came back!'

'You did it and came back. Your grandfather would be proud of you.'

Turning to Zander, Gabby smiled at the thought. Imagined her much-loved gramps patting her on the shoulder, a beaming smile on his face.

'I did it!' she repeated. 'I did it. I did it. *I did it!*'

And before either of them knew what was happening Zander had caught her around the waist and was twirling her round and round, both of them laughing like loons. Eventually he placed her on the sand gently and looked down into her eyes.

Heaven help her, all she wanted to do was kiss him. But she knew she mustn't. Even though right now, in the moment, she couldn't remember why it was bad idea. Adrenaline rush—that was all it was.

Who knew whether common sense would have prevailed? It wasn't put to the test, because a man approached them. Young, long hair, tanned, a happy smile, a surfboard under his arm.

'Gabby? I am Pedro. We spoke earlier. I am your surf instructor.'

'Fantastic! Hi, Pedro. This is Zander.'

'Pleased to meet you.'

A few preliminaries later and Pedro smiled again. 'Right. Time to choose your board and get you wetsuited up.'

Exhilaration still rushed through Gabby's whole body as she listened to him, still hardly able to believe that she had swum in the sea and was about to go back in.

Pedro was speaking. 'Before we go into the water, there are various techniques you need to practise on the sand. Paddling out. Popping up. Then we will move into the water, and I hope by the end of the afternoon you'll have caught your first wave!'

All her worries seemed to have dissipated—even the idea of catching a wave didn't faze her.

Her jubilation continued throughout the lesson, enhanced by watching Zander, his lithe movements and natural affinity for the surfboard. Something warmed inside her as she saw how carefree he looked, saw the look of concentration on his face, the smile that heated her skin with an intensity equal to the afternoon sun's rays, his deft, impatient movements as he pushed his hand through his sea-sprayed hair.

All of it gave her a funny little thrill of happiness, a sense of freedom—as if just for the day she was a different Gabby, one who had shed worry and caution.

The finale came when Pedro took them further out into the waves to put everything they had learnt into action. Zander lay on his board, his dark eyes intent and focused on the waves in assessment as he paddled. He bobbed, and then Pedro gave a small grunt of appreciation as Zander spotted the white-water wave, rode it and popped up.

'Like a pro, Zander! Way to go!' Pedro fist-pumped the air as Zander rode the wave in and then he turned to Gabby. 'Are you ready?'

'Yes!' Whether she was able was a different matter.

Zander grinned at her, reached out and took her hand in his. 'You've got this. I know you have.'

His voice was deep and genuine and his touch imbued her with confidence. The glint of appreciation in his blue eyes pumped her veins with a belief that she could do anything.

Grabbing her board, she headed out into the water, the sea swirling around her calves and then her thighs. She stood and let some white-water roll by, then closed her eyes as she tried to do as Pedro had instructed—get a feel for the rhythm and power of the waves. She held her surfboard in position, nose towards the waves.

OK. Now do this thing.

She identified a suitable incoming block of white water, took a deep breath and turned to face the shore. She lay on her board and paddled, focused. As the wave took the board and surged forward she stopped paddling, put her hands on the board, pushed up and popped her feet beneath her and did her best to stand and balance her weight.

As the surfboard washed on to shore she half fell, half leapt off, her muscle ache defeated by sheer exhilaration. 'I did it. I did it. I did it! *Again!*'

Pedro high-fived her and Gabby made no attempt to disguise her happiness, turning to Zander.

'At the risk of repeating myself—I did it! I did it! I did it! I did it! I caught a wave!'

'You did. You were amazing. Utterly incredible. How about we celebrate with a picnic on the beach?'

She looked around her. The rays of the setting sun cast a miasma of orange on the sand, their glow in direct contrast to the darkening dusky blue of the sea. Music emitted from the restaurants that lined the promenade above them, and the hum of conversation and laughter vibrated in the air. Lights twinkled into being, more than sufficient to combat the incoming dusk and cast an ambient illumination.

The whole idea of a picnic was impossibly romantic. With the emphasis on impossibly. The day might have had a dreamlike quality, but Zander was not the man of her dreams—not her Mr Right. Her Mr Right was a nice, ordinary bloke, not a drop-dead gorgeous, immensely successful multimillionaire.

Zander had been unattainable when she was a teenager and he was even more unattainable now.

He was too good-looking, too rich...too *much.* His world was not hers. His goal in life was to achieve even more wealth and boardroom triumph. His aura, his presence, would overwhelm her.

But today he had proved himself a friend—so, whilst romance wasn't on the cards, surely there was no danger in the enjoyment of each other's company.

'A picnic sounds awesome.'

'Leave it with me. Once we've changed, I'll sort it.'

CHAPTER NINE

ZANDER LOOKED AROUND the small but excellently stocked supermarket Pedro had recommended, chose his items carefully, then added a bottle of full-bodied red and two plastic wine glasses to his basket. He wondered why he had suggested a picnic at all.

He tried to tell himself it was simply a ploy to put off their return to the villa, where he might be tempted to check in with the office. But deep down he knew that he was only kidding himself. Standing there on the beach, seeing Gabby's joy in her achievements, still buzzing himself from the thrill of riding the waves, he had wanted to prolong the moment for as long as he could.

Friends had picnics all the time. One picnic—what could be the harm in that?

The answer arrived all too soon. As he made his way back to the beach, down the rickety wooden stairs towards where Gabby sat in the dusk, he stopped and caught his breath. Right now he wished with a deep gut-wrenching twist of desire that this was a fun fling for real, that the charade could be true.

But that wasn't possible. So instead he'd try to be a fun friend.

Arriving next to her, he placed the bags down and retrieved the newly purchased tartan picnic blanket, shaking it out with a theatrical flourish.

'I have come laden with food and drink, so I hope you're hungry.'

She rose to her feet and gave an exaggerated wince. 'I am definitely ravenous—and muscles I never knew existed ache! This looks incredible.'

Minutes later they had unpacked olives and bread, cold meats—*presunto* and *paio*, which the lady in the shop had explained to be smoked ham and smoked pork loin—a selection of cheese and some sardine pâté. *Batatas fritas*—chips—and pastries completed the spread.

Zander poured the wine and raised his glass. 'What shall we drink to?'

'To today. It's been amazing. I'm still buzzing.'

'Me, too.'

The feel of the sun on his skin, the cold salt spray of the water, the challenge of trying to master the surfboard and the waves had brought a surge of adrenaline that differed from the thrill of work, the buzz of a business deal. But, more than that, he'd felt pride in Gabby, in the way she'd faced, tackled and taken down her fears.

'Would you do it again?'

Her face clouded a little as she took a contemplative bite of a gleaming black olive. 'I don't know. Today feels like stolen time in some ways—as though it wasn't real. Wasn't me. Those feelings when I swam in the sea, when I caught the wave... *Exhilaration* doesn't do it justice as a description. There was that total sense of freedom, and for a transient second feeling in control of nature. I felt invincible.'

'A natural high?' Not the right words; he knew that immediately as her eyes dimmed in the evening light.

'I hadn't thought of it like that.' The idea clearly troubled her.

He frowned. 'There's nothing wrong with that. It's a great feeling.'

'That gets harder to achieve each time you seek it.' Her voice soft now. 'To start with, it's something small, and then that's not enough any more, so you need more and more to get that high. I'd have to swim the Channel, surf the most dangerous coast. And that's not me—I'm happy I managed to catch a wave. I think I'll stop there.' She spread some pâté on bread. 'What about you?' Her smile held a hint of sadness. 'Have you changed your mind? Are you going to set your sights on becoming a champion surfer?'

'No. I loved it, but I really don't have time to surf regularly.' Though now, sitting there, he felt a sudden uncharacteristic regret strike and had to remind himself. 'I get a buzz, a natural high, from success—from winning a deal, helping a client to succeed. I'll stick to that.'

'But, like I said, each time that goal becomes harder, and you need to achieve more to get that buzz. Surely in the end nothing will satisfy that craving except global domination?'

'You make ambition sound like an addiction. Maybe it is—but not a destructive one. Yes, I *would* like to achieve global success—I don't think that's a problem.' Not any more. But it had been once. His ambition had shown up the flaws his relationship with Claudia, but it would never be a problem again—he would never hurt anyone again—he'd make sure of that. 'I love my job and I am proud of my company. For me ambition, moving the goalposts, is a *good* thing. Else you stagnate.'

'Being content with what you have is not stagnation. I am happy with where I am, with what I have. I couldn't keep up with your level of ambition, your drive to succeed.'

Further confirmation that relationships and ambition didn't mix. 'We all have different contentment levels and different motivations.'

'That's true. And I'm sorry—I truly didn't mean to criticise your achievements. Your success is phenomenal.' A sudden smile illuminated her face. 'Tell me about it. How you did it.'

'Too dull.'

'No, it isn't. I want to know.'

Her voice sounded sincere, her enormous hazel eyes were focused on his face, and he figured, *Why not?*

'I wanted to succeed, but I also wanted to help other people set up their own businesses. Anyone. Not just people with expensive college backgrounds and loads of money. Anyone with an idea and the drive to achieve it. I'd been working in a bank. I went straight there after A levels.'

A levels had been incredibly hard for him and his learning curve as he'd tried to figure out dyslexia and a whole new world of study. But he'd got straight As—an achievement he still felt proud about.

'I decided university wasn't for me. And, given Claudia and I were already engaged, work seemed a sensible option.'

'Do you regret not going to university?'

'I'm not sure. I don't think it has impacted my life dramatically, but I would have liked the opportunity to spend three years studying something I felt passionate about. But at the time it seemed like a step too far.'

She nodded in understanding. 'So what happened next?'

'I did well at the bank. I'd always found numbers easy and I was interested in the business side of it all. But what I learnt was how many people there were out there who couldn't get a loan because they didn't have enough capital or a guarantor, or their ideas were too risky. That didn't seem right to me. So what I wanted to do was set up a consultancy firm that helped them—and, at the risk of sounding arrogant, I knew I would be able to make a go of it.'

After Claudia died. After those terrible months

when the sickness had moved in with inexorable, insidious finality.

'I decided to try to do just that. So I liquidated everything and worked out of—and lived in—a tiny rented garage.'

Of course his parents and his sisters had offered him a roof and help, but it had seemed vital to him that he achieve it all on his own.

'It was a lot…but it worked. I'd found a niche. There are so many people out there with innovative, fantastic ideas. I provided finance and advice and help, and it took off. I worked every hour I could, so I could fit around different time zones. It was a mad time.'

'And a confusing one, I imagine. A lot of that drive and energy must have been fuelled by grief.'

'Mostly I think I was driven by my own ambition.'

'I don't believe that. Claudia's illness, the tragedy of losing her, must have been beyond awful.'

'It was hard.'

He'd been there for her every minute, taken unpaid compassionate leave, tried to do everything he could to somehow mitigate the sheer tragedy. To help Claudia come to terms with her illness and navigate the acceptance that she had only months to live.

'I did my best. She wanted to live the time she had left to the fullest, but it was hard as she got weaker. We tried. I took her to Paris because we'd never been, and to Disneyland. We watched all the films she'd always wanted to.'

As he spoke he realised he'd never shared those bittersweet, tragic months with anyone—hadn't been able to, given the aftermath of his betrayal. But now, sitting on the green-and-orange-plaid rug in the moonlight, it felt cathartic, and he knew it was something to do with Gabby, with her ability to listen and her warmth.

'It sounds like you made her last months happy.'

He shook his head. 'Then weeks after she died I started my business. I'm not proud of that, but there it is.'

'You *should* be proud—Claudia would be, I'm sure. I wish she could have seen it, been part of it,' she said simply. 'I hope that somehow, some-where, she can.'

'It wouldn't make her proud. Why *would* it?' The words were tinged with bitterness and he sipped his wine, hoped the rich spiciness would remove the taste, but knew nothing could.

'Because she loved you. She'd want you to be happy, to have achieved your dream.'

Suddenly he couldn't let her believe that. He wouldn't share the whole truth—couldn't betray Claudia's memory—but he could at least burst the bubble that painted him as someone he wasn't.

'It wasn't her dream,' he stated. The words had never before been uttered, and they felt full of portent. 'Claudia didn't share this dream, this ambition. And so it took her death for me to get all my wealth and success. The worst thing of all is that I have enjoyed it—every step of my path to success. I've loved it all. So what sort of man does that make me? No need to answer that. It makes me a number-one bastard.'

There was a long silence. He kept his eyes on the sea, rougher now, the dark waves crested by moonlight.

Then, 'No, it doesn't.'

'That's easy for you to say.'

'Actually, it isn't easy. Because I know how you feel. I *know*.'

Her voice was low, the words caught by the

light evening breeze. The dusk had deepened and the warm night air held a different scent now. Cooking smells, sea spray, deeper and stronger.

'I know how it feels for a life to benefit from a death.'

Her tone was weighted with sadness and he moved closer to her so they sat shoulder to shoulder.

'*My* life. My mother was an addict. Drink, drugs... She was the all-time party girl. And becoming a parent didn't make any difference to her at all. She just took me along for the ride. My father was a drug dealer, a criminal... He eventually died in a prison brawl. Not that I ever knew him. My mother had moved on by then. She broke my grandparents' hearts—only came home when she needed money or when she needed somewhere to dump me. Sometimes it was a day, sometimes a week, sometimes a month.'

Zander was sure he heard the crack of his heart as a surge of impotent anger coursed through his body for tiny Gabby, tossed from pillar to post, never knowing where she would be from one minute to the next. No wonder she craved security.

'Anyway… When I was seven she left me with Gran and Gramps and she didn't come back. Eventually we were told that she'd died—overdosed. And you know what stinks? When I found out, my first emotion, my first thought, was, maybe I can stay here. With my grandparents. Where there is food and safety and security. So if *you're* a bastard, what does that make me?'

The words froze him in his tracks. They were an echo of his own feelings, only so very different.

'It makes you *human*. Gabby, you were a child. Your mother—the one person in the world who should have put you first, cared for you—didn't or couldn't give you the fundamental safety you deserved. It was a completely natural reaction. There is no fault.'

'That is logic speaking—but it doesn't change the burn of guilt inside me. For better or worse she was my mother, but her death benefited me. Gave me security, love and a home. So I understand how you feel about Claudia and it's a sucky feeling. But I'm sure that Claudia wouldn't begrudge you your success or blame you for it. She loved you and you loved her. Nothing is more important than that. I'm not sure my mother and I even had that.'

Only Gabby still didn't know the full truth. Once he and Claudia *had* loved each other, but his love had faded, withered, had not been strong enough to withstand their different approaches to life. But that was his cross to bear, and more important right now was Gabby—Gabby, who must have had such complex feelings for her mother.

He knew empty platitudes would be rightly rejected as inadequate, and he thought carefully before he spoke. 'I can't pretend to know how your mother felt, but addiction is a very terrible thing. It changes people—changes their priorities, their very nature. It can make them choose actions they know to be wrong.'

She nodded. 'I know. I've done a lot of research into it. But I do wish I'd been worth enough to her for her to try to turn it all around. Wish I'd been good enough'

'No one could have been good enough—it wasn't a flaw in you, it was a fault in her.'

'It didn't feel like that.'

He wondered if it still didn't.

'And still I wish that my first reaction to her death had been different.'

'I think that your mother would have understood, and she'd be happy that you ended up with love and security. I don't think she would begrudge you that, either.'

'Thank you. I mean that.' She shook her head. 'I can't believe I'm even talking about her. I never do, really. It upsets Gran and it makes me feel guilty.'

'You told me to make me feel better, and I appreciate that. Thank you.'

For a long moment they sat, and slowly the atmosphere began to morph and shimmer. His whole being was acutely aware of her closeness, her warmth and beauty.

She caught her breath. 'That's what friends are for.'

'Yes.' He turned to look at her, her chestnut hair sheened by moonlight, her features dappled by the beams casting them into shade and brightness. 'Problem is, right now I don't feel like just a friend.'

Her hazel eyes were luminous in the moonbeams as she twisted a strand of hair around her finger. 'So…like a friend…with benefits?'

Her voice was small, but clear, her gaze unwavering, and now the awareness that had simmered, muted by the sheer emotional warmth of their conversation, shifted, almost as if the moon's haze had cast a sparkling net of magical awareness around them.

'What sort of benefits did you have in mind?'

Now she smiled—a slow, almost languorous smile. 'I'm thinking of the exact type of benefits *you* have in mind.'

All he wanted to do was kiss her, but some innate sense of honour pulled him back, kept him still.

'Unless I've got this all wrong?' Hurt, fear of rejection, crossed her eyes.

She made to move backwards and instantly he reached out, covering her hand in his.

'No! You haven't got it wrong. *Jeez.* I want this. I want you more than I can say. But I need to be sure you want it, too. You said that fun flings aren't your thing, that you don't want to feel second-best. I don't want you to feel like that.'

'I don't. This isn't about being second-best—this is about what we both want in the here and now.' Her hand picked up some sand, trickled it through her fingers. 'For once I don't want to be cautious—the one who clings to the shore, who won't take a risk, won't have fun. For once

I want to let go. Just for a weekend. I want to break free from common sense and reason and all the shibboleths and worries that govern my life. One weekend. That doesn't complicate anything.'

His brain made a last-ditch attempt to tell him that it wasn't that easy—that this would complicate everything—but he shut it down. One weekend—what could be wrong with that?

'Are you sure?' His breath caught in his lungs as he waited for her answer. 'Sure this is what you want?

CHAPTER TEN

GABBY STARED INTO his eyes, then glanced around the beach, wanting to imprint it for ever on her memory. Then she looked back at Zander. Took in every detail. The darkness of his blue-grey eyes, the contained, controlled aura of desire that she knew was for her, and revelled in that knowledge.

'I'm sure. One hundred per cent.' She could see doubt fighting desire in his stance. 'You can be my Mr Right for the Weekend.'

For a second inexplicable sadness touched her, but then she pushed it away. Zander could not be her Mr Right for Ever. His life goals were utterly different from hers—and, of more importance perhaps, she couldn't keep up with him. She wasn't in his league and it wasn't a league she wanted to be in—not a world she wanted to be part of. Lord knew she loved her niche, the place in the world she'd forged and carved out for herself. Secure, safe… A place where she could be content.

But right now that didn't matter—nothing mattered except the here and now, and for once she was going to grab the moment. And him.

'I want this. I want *you.*'

And finally he smiled and her heart soared.

'Then what are we waiting for? It would be my pleasure. *Our* pleasure, in fact.'

She could hear the rough edge of desire in his voice and it thrilled her. His eyes, molten in the moonlight, were completely focused on her as he leant forward and brushed his lips across hers with a tantalising slowness, caressing her shoulders. Her skin shivered under his touch and desire surged inside her in a swirling vortex of need that only he could assuage.

She couldn't hold back the moan of protest when he pulled away.

'We need to go. Get back to the villa.'

Together, their fingers made clumsy by the sheer need for speed, they cleared away the remnants of their picnic, rolled up the rug and half walked, half ran up the beach to where the lighted streets still showed couples out for a stroll, bars lit up and where there was the sound of late-night diners, laughter and the hum of conversation.

Within minutes he'd found a taxi, tugged her towards it and their journey began. A silent journey, broken only by a few courteous platitudes to the driver. There was no need for words to each other, nothing to say that could eclipse the mounting anticipation inside her. Not a single doubt was allowed to surface—she knew that she couldn't stop now, propelled by a desire so deep, so consuming, it wouldn't be possible to deny it.

As she alighted from the taxi she felt as though she was walking through a sea of sensation. Every sound was magnified, every chirp of a cricket, every rustle of a tree's branches in the wind. The breeze lifted her hair against the nape. Her skin was supersensitive. Her heartbeat pounded in her ears as Zander pulled her into his arms and kissed her—a deep searing kiss in which their mutual passion met and matched, a kiss that branded her very soul.

Time lost meaning, and it could have been minutes or hours that they stood lip-locked, surrounded by the late-night garden scents. But finally he took her hand and they walked unsteadily towards the front door.

Once inside they wasted no time, practically sprinting for the stairs, and she gave a small laugh of relief as they reached the mezzanine level—until he dropped an expletive.

'What?'

'I haven't got any protection...'

'It doesn't matter. I'm on the pill.'

She had remained on it after her split with Steve, as it regulated her periods. It was a decision she had been unsure about, but now she welcomed it with a wash of relief, matched by Zander's and shown in the force of his answer when she explained.

And then the need for words was over; his expression said it all, and he was utterly focused, almost reverent, as he gently pushed the straps of her dress down, bent his head and whispered kisses across her shoulder. How was it possible to feel boneless, to be so caught up, so focused on the thrills that ricocheted through her?

She reached out in wonder. Finally this was allowed—to slide her hands under the soft fabric of his T-shirt and feel the muscular solidity of his chest, to rest her palm over the accelerated beat of his heart. And then he was kissing her again, and Gabby gave herself up to the sensory onslaught...

Zander opened his eyes and stared up at the whitewashed ceiling, aware of the rays of bright sunshine that filtered through the slatted blinds they had forgotten to close properly. A feeling of immense well-being filled him—an urge to throw open the windows and sing. Instead he shifted slightly, aware that next to him Gabby still slept.

For a long moment he looked down at her and marvelled at the sheer joy they had experienced just hours before. Passion, laughter, discovery and a generosity that still startled him. Now she lay curled on her side, her impossibly long eyelashes on show, one hand tucked under her cheek.

As quietly as he could, he slipped from the bed, closed the shutters so she could sleep on and tiptoed downstairs, determined to produce a spectacular breakfast.

Half an hour later her head appeared over the banister. 'That smells divine!'

'Bacon, eggs, pastries, coffee, toast. They

stocked the kitchen in style. I figure we burned off a whole load of calories. I also figure we need a whole load more energy for what I have in mind.'

An endearing blush and a wicked smile greeted this, and she padded downstairs dressed in an oversized T-shirt. Her hair cascaded wildly to her shoulders and his heart did a funny little dip.

Whoa, Zander. Any other bit of his anatomy, sure, but his heart really did *not* need to get involved.

Turning away, he concentrated on breakfast and on the plunge of the cafetière, and the sheer unfamiliarity of cooking for two smote him. It was a reminder that this was not normal—it was a capsule of time outside reality and away from the usual slipstream of their lives.

'So.' He placed a heaped plate in front of her. 'What's our plan for the day?'

'Well, we could follow our old plan—visit the fairy-tale castle or the palace...' Reaching out, she concentrated on buttering a piece of toast, her eyes on the knife as if the whole enterprise was a complicated military strategy. 'Or we could stay here. Play board games, read books, drink coffee, cook...and anything else that takes our fancy.' A small shrug. 'Have a complete break from the world.'

The phrase was an echo of his earlier thoughts.

Zander poured more coffee, shocked at how very much the idea appealed. Never before had he embraced the idea of doing nothing, let alone doing it wrapped in cosy intimacy.

A small alarm bell started to sound. 'Are you sure? I saw yesterday how enthusiastic you were about the castle and the whole history of Sintra.'

'I was. I am. But...'

Her cheeks flushed and he couldn't help but smile. 'But you figure there are better activities on offer than sightseeing?'

'Well...now that you mention it...'

His brain shut off the growing siren that urged caution and his vocal cords jumped into action. 'A complete break from the world sounds good. The castle will be there another day.'

Whereas whatever was happening here had a time limit. It was a reminder to himself—a justification as to *why* he wanted to spend the next two days cocooned with Gabby in the villa. After all, once they went back to England normal life would resume. The opening of an office in New York, deals and clients and business growth—

that was where his focus had to be. But suddenly he didn't want to think about that.

'I vote we stay right here. And I have a brilliant idea. Let's go back to bed.'

'Works for me.'

And so started a day unlike any Zander had experienced before—a day when time seemed to lose meaning as they alternated between conversations about films and books and comfortable silence, as they played Monopoly and ate gigantic ham-and-cheese toasties in bed.

'It's been an amazing day,' he said softly as the night drew in and he opened a bottle of champagne.

'Yes, it has. I'll definitely be putting this day in my treasure trove.'

Handing her a frothing glass, he settled next to where she was curled up on the sofa, dressed in a fluffy dressing gown. 'Treasure trove?'

'It's something Gran came up with when I was a child. It was hard, knowing that the time I spent with her and Gramps could be snatched away at any time. And I never knew if Mum would bring me back again or not. So Gran said we should make a treasure trove of memories. Special things that I could treasure and take out and remember when I needed them. It was a brilliant idea. When things were tough I'd imagine opening the treasure trove and there they'd be. I'd lose myself in the memories.'

Her eyes were looking into the past now, and he wondered how bad it had been. 'I'm guessing it was pretty tough,' he said.

'Yes, sometimes it was.' Her voice was flat, matter-of-fact, and then she smiled. 'But there were some good memories, and that's where the treasure trove came in. When good things happened I'd make sure to imprint every second on my mind and I'd imagine putting the memory into a special box. And now it's a habit I've got into. It helps sometimes—when things go wrong it's good to remember there were happy times. Sometimes Gran and I sit and remember Gramps, look into our treasure troves of memories of him.'

Zander watched Gabby and saw the affection on her face. 'Your gran sounds like a really special person.'

'She is. I'd do anything for her. Gran is the best person I know. And Gramps was pretty impressive, too. Life wasn't always easy for them but they never gave up, never despaired. Gran

says it's because they had each other. She says
Gramps was her rock, and the knowledge that
their love was indestructible gave them both
strength in the dark times. One day I hope I can
find that kind of love, but I realise it's probably
a pipe dream.'

'Why?' Conflicting emotions hit him. Right
now the idea of Gabby with the love of her life
didn't sit well with him—in fact the idea of
Gabby with *anyone* else caused a knot of anger
in his gut. Dog in the manger, or what? He told
himself that of *course* he wanted her to have
what she wanted.

'You're only twenty-nine. There's plenty of
time to find Mr Right.'

'Even if I find him I'd have to figure out how
to keep him, how to maintain the relationship.'

'You make it sound like a car.'

'A relationship *is* like a car—Gran told me she
and Gramps had to work at theirs. Sometimes
it needs fuel, sometimes it needs fine-tuning,
sometimes it needs a polish.'

'So you *do* know what you're doing?'

'Nope.' She shook her head, chestnut strands
shaking in emphasis. 'In real life I have no clue
how to look after a car, and I don't have any idea

with relationships, either. Been there and have the T-shirt.'

'What went wrong?'

'I think I wanted it to work *too* much. Then I couldn't figure out how to *make* it work, and the harder I tried the more panicked I became. That had a knock-on effect and made me madly insecure and needy. That made both Steve *and* Miles run for the hills—or rather run to other women.'

Her tone was light, but he knew how hurt she must have been. 'Whoa... Hold on a minute. That was their fault—they were the ones who were wrong, not you.'

'I know. I get that. And to be fair they got that, too—they both did feel really bad about their behaviour. They accepted complete responsibility...gave me the whole "it's not you, it's me" spiel.'

'They got *that* right,' he pointed out and heard the anger in his voice. It was an anger aimed not at Gabby, but at the unknown Steve and Miles. Anger at how they must have made her feel. Gabby's mother had made her feel not good enough, and they had added to that. 'They were schmucks. They weren't worth it and they weren't worthy of you. You're well rid of them.'

'I tell myself that, but I do also accept that it's possible that there isn't a Mr Right out there for me. Both Steve and Miles seemed so right—good, normal, ordinary blokes.' She sipped her champagne and then smiled. 'Don't get me wrong—I'm happy on my own. I love my job and I have security, a home, food on the table, consistency. And I have Gran—which is amazing, given she's ninety. I'm lucky and I know that.'

Yet once her grandmother passed on, and in the scheme of things that could happen sooner rather than later, Gabby would be alone. No wonder she wanted a family, and had wanted her relationships with Steve and Miles to work out too much.

Without thought, Zander shifted a little closer to her and she rested her head on his shoulder.

'Anyway,' she said. 'Enough about me. Let's talk about you.'

'What do you want to know?'

'What were you like as a child? What did you want to be when you grew up?'

'That's easy. I wanted to be a success. Simple as that. I didn't care how I did it or what I did—I wanted success.'

She frowned. 'So you were always ambitious?

It's funny—I don't remember that about you at school.'

'Sixth form was a strange time for me.'

It was the time when he'd just started seeing Claudia. He had been unable to read, but had been incredibly popular—a success on the sporting field, a cool kid, a rebel who had hardly any qualifications but seemingly didn't care. A kid on the path to success of the wrong type. Then had come the dyslexia diagnosis—a turning point and a time when everything had changed for him. A vista of possibilities had opened up, and his determination and drive had been focused around conquering the written word.

His relationship with Claudia had deepened at a time when his ambition had been muted, and with hindsight he could see that perhaps it meant Claudia hadn't known the real Zander. And perhaps he hadn't known the real Claudia—he had been grateful she had gone out with him, someone 'stupid', but in reality she had been happy to go out with someone cool. But that didn't answer Gabby's question.

'I was always determined to succeed. I think because my sisters had set the bar so high and I hated being the stupid one. I was always intent on equalling them.'

Her forehead creased in thought and then she sighed. 'Yet you gave up that dream for Claudia because you loved her. You were happy to accept that her dreams were different. *That* is how relationships work—two people willing to compromise. You obviously understood the maintenance manual. That's why you truly don't need to feel guilt because you achieved success after her death.'

The words hit him like individual pellets and he had to force himself not to wince with each blow. Yet she sensed something; it clearly hadn't been possible to keep the tension from his body.

'I'm sorry. I shouldn't have reminded you.' Her voice was small, sounding suddenly almost defeated. 'Of what you've lost.'

Jeez. Each word poured salt into the wound, and for a moment he hesitated, wondered if he could admit the truth, air his guilt and the baseness of his soul to her. But that wasn't the issue. Sharing his flaws meant a betrayal of Claudia. It would humiliate her memory.

'You haven't.'

How to explain that he couldn't talk about

Claudia? Not without conjuring up all his guilt and sadness…not without confessing that in fact he'd had no idea at all about relationship maintenance or compromise. That in fact his love hadn't survived marriage, living together, a real relationship.

He could see compassion in Gabby's eyes, along with a frisson of sadness, and then she shifted, moved in and kissed him softly on the lips. Her sympathy was so wrong he moved away. Then he saw hurt in her eyes and wished it were possible to kick himself round the whole of Sintra.

'Gabby…?'

'It's fine. Really.'

It wasn't, but he didn't have a clue how to make it better. Whatever he said would make it worse, because he couldn't tell her the truth.

'What did you want to be when you grew up?' As a question it was abrupt, gauche, stupid, but it was all he could come up with. 'Did you always want to be a librarian?'

For a moment he thought she wouldn't answer, then she shrugged, accepted the conversational gambit. 'I wanted to be safe. I still do. You want success—I want security. As a child I don't think

I much cared how I got it, but as I grew older I did realise I had a choice. My priority was and is a regular income. Though I did once toy with the idea of being a writer.' She said it as though the idea was a crazy one.

'What did you want to write?'

'Happy stories,' she said without hesitation. 'But also stories that make you think. For kids. Books were an incredible solace for me, growing up—they allowed me to escape from a difficult world into a fantasy one. I used to imagine the pages literally swallowing me up. And I was glad of it. I'm sorry that you didn't have that.'

He shrugged. 'Some people say you can't miss what you never had, but I think what's worse is desperately wanting something you *can't* have. I used to think I'd wish away my soul if I could just decipher the meaningless jumble of shapes that everyone else could read.'

Gabby moved back closer to him, so close a silken strand of her hair brushed his cheek. 'That truly sucks.'

'Yeah. But, hey, somehow the conversation seems to have come back to me. What about you? Do you still want to write a book?'

'No. There wouldn't be any point.'

'Why not?'

'Because I'd rather focus on a job that brings me money.' She paused. 'Like this one.'

It was a timely reminder to them both that this was a job—that these few days were not real.

He took a breath. 'Perhaps writing a book would make you money.'

'Unlikely. The chance of success in the current competitive market is minuscule.'

'But if you don't try you won't succeed for sure. Why not write in your spare time? Not for the money, but for the kudos of publication. You already have a job and security.'

'Exactly. I've achieved the important things. The whole "write a children's book" thing was just a daft dream.'

'Dreams are important.'

'Sure they are—but not dreams that can't be achieved and will most likely open you up to rejection.'

'But you might get accepted.'

'Unlikely—and getting rejected sucks. So I can't see the point of inviting it.'

'But—'

'There is no *but*. Subject closed. Let's not spoil this with a pointless argument.'

Stop. Quit.

Gabby was right. Yet he couldn't shake the idea that he was missing something, and he asked a question on instinct. 'You've already written it, haven't you?'

There was a silence. Then a shrug. 'Yes. Though I don't know how you figured that out.'

Instinct, and the knowledge of Gabby he had somehow garnered. 'Then why not send it out?'

'I didn't write it for publication. I wrote it for me.' A small shrug and then, 'Maybe if I ever figure out relationships and have children, I'll read it to them.'

Children. The word was another reminder of just how different he and Gabby were. Gabby could picture a world where she was a parent— she actively wanted that responsibility. Zander couldn't and didn't. But right now that didn't matter.

'Anyway...' She said the word with finality. 'Can we change the subject?

He bit down on his instinct to urge her to send her story off, to do what *he* would do— strive after success. Gabby had been deemed not good enough by her mother, not good enough to give up her lifestyle for. She had been terrified she wouldn't be good enough to be kept by her grandparents, and she believed she had played a part in both her relationships ending in infidelity. Perhaps it was no wonder she didn't want to risk being judged not good enough again.

No wonder she wanted to settle for an 'ordinary' bloke. Maybe the best thing he could do was tell her that *he* thought she was good enough.

'Yes, we can. But first I want to say I believe that those children of yours will be really lucky. To have the chance to listen to your story, but most of all to have you as a mum.'

For a second he'd have sworn a tear glistened on the end of one of those impossibly long eyelashes, but then she pulled him towards her and her generous lips curved into a smile of sheer beauty.

'You say the loveliest things. But now I think it's time to stop talking.'

He laughed, 'And show you some action?'

'Absolutely.'

CHAPTER ELEVEN

GABBY ROLLED OVER, felt the last vestige of sleep slip away from her and tried to hold on to it. She knew that she didn't want to wake up just yet.

Drowsily she reached out a hand, expecting to encounter Zander's warm, comforting bulk next to her. Instead her hand met cool sheets and now she *did* open her eyes. Remembered. This was it. The morning of their flight back. She needed to be up and packing. It was over.

A queasily familiar sense of impending unhappiness washed over her but she forced herself to jump out of bed instantly, to infuse her movements with purpose even as memory strummed a chord. This was akin to how she'd felt as a child, when her mother had returned to pick her up from her grandparents'. She'd packed her suitcase then with the same dread, with the knowledge that her safe time was over and she didn't know when or even if it would come again.

To her horror, this was actually *worse*. Back

then there had been hope—even the probability that she would return, perhaps in days, perhaps in months. But this was different. This would never happen again. She'd asked him to be her Mr Right for the Weekend—and the weekend was over.

But she would not, *could* not regret it. Their moment had been joyous and joyful—and, dammit, she'd had *fun*. So now she would act with dignity and she would not repine.

Gabby snapped her suitcase shut and switched on her brightest smile, preparing to descend from the mezzanine and face him.

'Good morning!' Her words came out too cheerful, too shiny and bright, but he didn't comment.

'Good morning.'

His voice was pleasant, courteous—and so formal. Hurt twanged her nerves. The man she had come to know over the past forty-eight hours had vanished as completely as a mirage in the desert. That Zander had gone and she would never see that aspect of him again.

'I've made coffee if you would like some.'

'Thank you.'

For a moment she wondered if he'd ask if she

took milk or sugar—perhaps the past two days had been a figment of her fevered imagination. He handed her the mug with exaggerated care, careful to avoid even a brush of their fingers. On the table his netbook was open, and she had little doubt he had already been in contact with his office.

The silence held a cloud of awkwardness and she forced herself to fill it. 'Hopefully the flight won't be delayed.'

'Hopefully not. We should leave within the next half hour, if that's OK with you.'

'Traffic shouldn't be too bad,' she stated, as if she had *any* knowledge of traffic congestion in Portugal. Oh, God—they'd gone full circle. Their break had started with stilted conversation and so it would end. As if the middle had been no more substantial than a dream.

They left the villa in silence and she forced herself to walk to the car without a backward glance. Better for it be preserved in her treasure trove of memories as a magical place untouched by shadows of regret.

The whole car journey consisted of her fight to remain still, to contain her agitation and to focus on the scenery as it whizzed past rather than on Zander. Yet she couldn't resist the occasional glance at his profile. His expression was unreadable—not even a hint of the man who'd just hours ago held her in his arms.

Anger suddenly sparked that he could be so calm, so uncaring—that he could switch off his emotions so easily. But then again his emotions hadn't been engaged, and in theory neither had hers. She shifted on her seat again, realising that now Zander's fingers were drumming a tattoo on the steering wheel. An apology hovered on her lips but she bit it back—she had nothing to apologise for.

Then in a smooth movement Zander put on the indicator and pulled into a lay-by. 'Is something wrong with the car?'

'No.'

He unclicked his seat belt and turned to face her. 'But *something* feels wrong. On the beach we decided to change the parameters of our relationship for the weekend, but we didn't stop to think about what would happen next. And now we're acting like strangers.' His shoulders lifted in a shrug as his lips tipped up ruefully. 'I'm not sure I even understand why, but I don't like it.'

Relief touched her that he didn't want this

stilted awkwardness, either. 'I guess we need to figure out how to go back to friendship.' *Right, Gabs. Because that worked out so well last time.* 'Or to a working relationship at least. You're paying me for a reason. We don't want to blow it now.' The reminder tasted bitter on her tongue.

He nodded but made no attempt to restart the car. Instead, his fingers continued to drum the wheel as he gazed ahead at the dusty vista of the road.

'There is another way,' he said finally. 'An option that has nothing to do with money. Whatever we decide I will pay you the agreed sum, because I'm paying you to convince my family that I have moved on. But, given that we are going to see a lot of each other until the wedding, we *could* make this into a *real* fun fling. Just for the next few weeks.'

'I...'

Yes! Hurry up and say yes, urged every instinct. *For heaven's sake, please don't think about it.* Even her brain chimed in. *Go on, it makes sense.*

She had made the decision on those sands to grab the moment. This was her chance to extend it. To continue to enjoy the benefits that she knew with every millimetre of her body were infinitely pleasurable.

Only her gut urged caution, informing her that it was too dangerous, that it would be too much.

But it was too late for that consideration. For the next few weeks their relationship charade had to continue regardless. That necessitated her being with Zander, and it would take a person with more willpower than she had to turn down the option of more time in his arms and in his bed.

'That would make sense,' she said, keeping her voice cool and calm, as if they were simply negotiating a simple additional clause to their deal. Though her tummy somersaulted with doubt and anticipation, relief and anxiety in equal measure.

'Good.'

His smile was warm, his body language relaxed—a return to the Zander she'd got to know over the past three days and she smiled back.

Now he did start the engine, and pulled out on to the road. They resumed their journey, still in silence, but this time it was a silence that spoke of relief, and of a disinclination to start any conversation that might convince them of the sheer idiocy of their decision.

Four days later

'Do I look all right? Does this work for a Grosvenor family lunch?' Gabby surveyed her reflection in the mirror in Zander's bedroom and then turned to look at Zander, who stood by the bed, smiling at her.

It occurred to Gabby that they'd both smiled a lot since she'd arrived the previous evening, and an illogical frisson of unease touched her. *Daft.* Smiling was a *good* thing, right?

'Hmm… I think I need to take a closer look.'

As he advanced towards her, she gestured at the simple patterned drop-waisted dress. 'I've gone for a casual, I've-tried-hard-but-not-too-hard look,' she explained.

He raised his eyebrows in genuine bemusement. 'You know that makes no sense, right?'

'It does to me. The point is, will your family think it's OK?'

'My family doesn't have a dress code.'

Now his smile had deepened, and she looked at him with a hint of suspicion as he stepped closer.

'But let me quickly check something on the back of your dress.'

She swivelled round and in one swift movement, he'd slipped the straps off her shoulders and bent down to kiss the nape of her neck.

'I think I'd better inspect *exactly* how you look,' he murmured, and now he tugged the zipper down.

Desire washed over her and without hesitation she turned and shimmied out of the dress...

Half an hour later Gabby shook her head as she tugged the dress back on, grabbed a pair of heels and slipped them on, too. 'I can't *believe* we did that. If we're late it is all *your* fault.' She regarded her reflection and groaned. 'Do you think they'll guess that we just...?' She waved a hand at the rumpled sheets.

Zander buttoned his shirt. 'We won't be late—and if they do, they do. It all adds verisimilitude to the charade.'

'Yes. Of course.' All inclination to laugh left her. Had he instigated the whole thing to enhance the charade?

His blue-grey eyes held concern. 'Gabs... That wasn't planned. It just happened.'

'I get that.'

But she wasn't sure she did—suddenly wasn't sure if she was overthinking, on the way to insecurity or neediness.

Rising, she glanced at her watch. 'We'd better go. I don't know London that well but, according to my phone app, it will take us at least forty-five minutes to get to Gemma's.'

In fact, the journey across London took just under that, and they pulled up outside Gemma's three-storey London house at the same time as Julia and her children.

'Hey, little bro,' she said.

But before Zander could reply, Freddy and Heidi tumbled out of the car.

'Uncle Zan-Zan! Look at my new game—it helps me read and it means I get to use a tablet.'

'Uncle Zan-Zan, tell Mum that isn't fair.' The little girl folded her arms. 'I think I should have one, too.'

Zander grinned, and as both children ran towards him he scooped Heidi up. 'You'll have to manage without, Heidi. How about I play a game with you later?'

Heidi squealed with laughter as he tickled her, and nodded. 'Hide and seek, Uncle Zan-Zan— and Monopoly. Please.' Turning, she looked across at Gabby. 'Are you Gabby?'

Gabby nodded.

'Are you Uncle Zan-Zan's girlfriend?'

'Yes, sweetheart, she is—and, now, enough questions. We need to go inside.'

With that, Julia swept everyone towards the front door, and minutes later they were inside. Unlike Zander's apartment, the house had a lived-in feel and a definite sense of personal taste. Gemma clearly favoured bold abstracts and warm wooden flooring. The hall held a collage of family photographs in black and white, and for a sudden moment Gabby felt a sense of aloneness, a stab of emotion that she acknowledged as envy.

Before she could dwell further, she saw Laura Grosvenor heading towards her. 'Gabby, how lovely to see you. You look fantastic—positively glowing! The sun has done you both good and I love your dress.'

'Thank you.'

Gabby returned the hug and again emotion swelled inside her—a sense of being an outsider looking in. She wanted *this*—the clear affection that existed in this family, the easy camaraderie, the jokes and the banter. Yearning tugged inside her, but she blinked it away. One day she would find Mr Right and she'd create this—have

children, laughter, family holidays, Christmases
with a turkey large enough to feed an army.

Once they were all seated around the large
wooden table in the state-of-the-art kitchen,
Gemma grinned at Gabby. 'OK. So tell us all
about Sintra. Was it fantastic?'

'It was absolutely amazing,' Gabby said, and
now there was no need to act her part. All she
had to do was tell the truth. 'Magical, in fact.'

'We even went surfing.' Zander held his arms
out and gestured for applause. 'Gabby and I
caught our first waves.'

'No way.'

'*Yes*, way.'

'And how many hours did he spend on his laptop or talking to the office?'

'None,' Zander said.

'*Definitely* no way.'

'Yup. Gabby will vouch for me.' Zander was
relaxed, his arm around her shoulders, and she
felt a bubble of happiness because for a moment
she truly felt she belonged.

'It's the truth. And he even came home early
from the office yesterday to meet me.'

'In that case we all need to drink to you,
Gabby.' Gemma rose to her feet and lifted her

glass. 'To Gabby, who has achieved the impossible. Cheers!'

And when Gaby saw the look of happiness on his mother's face, she understood why Zander had initiated the whole illusion.

The hours flew by. They ate a delicious simple home-cooked lasagne and a green salad, followed by a sumptuous cake that Gemma happily admitted was from the local patisserie. A boisterous game of hide-and-seek ensued, followed by a fiercely competitive game of Monopoly. Then the children were allowed to watch a film whilst the adults sat on the circle of sofas in the enormous living area.

'So,' Gemma said. 'Have you bought a dress for the wedding yet?'

'Not yet,' Gabby said and smiled. 'But that's not important—it's *your* dress that everyone will be interested in.'

Gemma shook her head. 'You wouldn't believe the fuss—all because Alessio can drive a car fast.'

Zander laughed, '*That* is a master understatement.'

'Pah!' Gemma waved a dismissive hand. 'Anyway, the point I was making is that the dress has been a massive drama. Loads of designers want the job! One up-and-coming woman—Hannah Colter—even sent me a free sample dress. Not a wedding dress, but it's beautiful. Actually—' she looked Gabby over with a critical eye '—it would be perfect for *you*.'

'I couldn't possibly...'

'Yes, you could. Hannah would be stoked at the publicity. Just come and look.'

Gabby glanced at Zander but he laughed and shook his head. 'No use appealing to me—I've never been able to get Gem to give up on an idea.'

Succumbing to the inevitable, Gabby followed Gemma up the stairs to a large and messy spare bedroom.

'This is the wedding room—or *wedding dumping ground* might be a better description.' Gemma headed to a large wardrobe, tugged the doors open, reached inside and pulled out a transparent zippered dress bag, through which Gabby could see the sparkle of shimmering material.

Qualms began to surface. Instinct informed her that the dress was most definitely not suitable—not her type, not her style. Not *her*. Too visible.

Oblivious to her dilemma, Gemma pulled the dress out and Gabby held back a small gasp. Hundreds of adjectives flooded her brain. *Magical, shimmery, delicate, gorgeous.*

'Right. Let's try it on,' Gemma stated.

And somehow, ten minutes later, Gabby was wearing it, staring at her reflection with shell-shocked eyes. Sleek and sleeveless, the dress left her shoulders and neckline bare, emphasising the slenderness of her waist before falling in a silvery, sparkling, sculpted waterfall to the floor.

'I...'

'You look like a fairy-tale princess. Decision made. It's yours.'

But this wasn't who she was—clad in designer gear, glittering for every eye to see. And yet... The wedding would mark the end of her time with Zander and, damn it—how did she want him to remember her? Like this or muted and neutral? The answer was absolute. Let his final memory of her be a dazzling one. Just once let her risk coming out of her shell for the occasion. Because after the wedding she would return to life as normal. It would be her final show and she'd make it a good one.

'If you're sure, then thank you.'

'I'm sure.' Gemma packed the dress back into its bag and handed it to her. 'Here you go. You may as well take it now.'

With that they returned downstairs, and soon after that the party dispersed.

'Your family are wonderful,' Gabby said as Zander started the car. 'I can see why you want to make them happy.'

By faking a relationship. With each moment it seemed increasingly important to remind herself of that. Fact and fiction were beginning to blur and she had to ensure she could see the defining line.

'So,' she said. 'What now? If you drop me at a Tube station, I can head back home. It's not that late.'

There was a pause as Zander drummed the steering wheel with his fingers—it was a trait she now recognised as his thinking trait.

'Actually...why not make a weekend of it?' he suggested slowly.

Gabby hesitated as instincts warred within her. Then, 'That sounds great. If we stop at a supermarket on the way back, I'll even cook dinner, if you want. I do a great fish pie and salad.'

She closed her eyes in silent despair. *Fish pie*

and salad? This was a man who could afford to dine out on caviar every night of the week.

But Zander smiled. 'Fish pie and salad sounds perfect.'

Zander pushed the trolley around the supermarket as Gabby chose items, enjoying the intent expression on her face, her ability to imbue such an everyday chore with interest.

'Do you have any dill?' she asked.

'I think you should work on the assumption that my cupboards are bare.'

Gabby looked up from the potatoes she was assessing. 'So how does *that* work? Presumably you need to eat. You don't have some sort of superpower that enables you to subsist on air?'

'Unfortunately not. I mostly eat out or get food delivered to the office. Also, every so often Mum descends and fills my freezer with homemade meals I can just heat up. I go to the local shop as and when I need staple items.'

Gabby grinned suddenly. 'Well, it doesn't seem to have done you any harm.'

The smile lit her face and tugged at his gut, causing an urge to pull her into his arms in the middle of aisle three and kiss her. *Not a good idea.* It was worrying enough that he'd suggested extending the weekend, decided to abandon the office in favour of her company.

So instead he said, 'Do you want me to look for anything?'

Gabby shook her head. 'I'm nearly done. All I need are ingredients for the salad.'

'Leave that to me.'

Half an hour later they carried the loaded bags into his kitchen, unpacked the ingredients and set to work.

'This is Gramps's recipe and I love it,' Gabby said as she selected a knife from the block and started to chop onions. 'When I was a kid I'd have it with ketchup and baked beans, but as I got older I figured out it was better without!' Reaching for the garlic, she looked up at him. 'What was *your* favourite childhood dish?'

'My mum's chicken casserole, closely followed by Dad's pork chops in cream with potato dauphinoise. We always ate together, so mealtimes were pretty noisy affairs.'

'Like today at Gemma's?'

'Yes.'

'You were lucky,' she said quietly, as the smell of sizzling onions pervaded the air. 'Sometimes I wished so hard for siblings, to be part of a "normal" family. And then I'd feel guilty, or I'd worry the social workers would think I'd be better off somewhere else.'

'Was that ever a possibility?'

'Gran and Gramps were in their seventies and there were concerns. So many visits and meetings and whispered conversations... I was constantly petrified I'd be taken away. Luckily we jumped through all the hoops, I played my part and there was a happy ending.'

Zander's heart went out to her. 'Did you *have* to play a part?'

'Yes! It was incredibly important that I came across as quiet and well-adjusted—a child who wouldn't cause any issues at all. Perhaps it was a good thing—it taught me to push down anger and grief and focus on the positive, on my goals in life. In truth it wasn't only the social workers I needed to convince—it was Gran and Gramps, as well.'

Zander frowned. 'But there must have been times when you didn't feel quiet or well-adjusted?'

'Sure, but I wasn't only worried about convincing the social workers. I was scared that they were right—that I would be too much for my grandparents, or that I would remind them too much of my mum. I was scared they would change their minds, and I was grateful they took me in. So I knew I had to be perfect.'

'Didn't you ever feel like being loud and noisy and letting your hair down?'

'Maybe years ago, but not any more. It's not in my nature now. I'm quite happy looking on whilst other people do that.'

Zander didn't believe her—he sensed that along with her grief and anger, Gabby had also stifled her joie de vivre and her sense of adventure.

'I've got an idea.' He glanced at his watch. 'How long does your fish pie need in the oven?'

'An hour.'

'Perfect. Then once you have it in, why don't we pop out for a predinner drink in the pub?'

'Sure. That sounds nice.'

As he mashed potatoes and shelled hard-boiled eggs, mixed a salad dressing and loaded the dishwasher, he hummed under his breath.

Gabby's eyes scrunched in suspicion. 'You look like Freddy did earlier, when he was planning on mischief.'

'Moi?' He opened his eyes wide in simulated

surprise. 'What mischief could I possibly be planning?'

'I don't know…' Opening the oven, she popped the fish pie in and he gestured to the door.

'Let's go.'

They walked the tree-lined streets, inhaling the smell of the nearby river, until he spotted what he was looking for—a pub a colleague had mentioned.

'Here we are.'

The pub exuded warmth. People had spilled out on to the street, glasses in hand, and the sound of music tumbled out to mix with the chatter and laughter. Once inside they headed to the bar, and Zander beamed as he saw the stage against one of the walls, plastered with posters of local bands.

'Look at that,' he said. 'Turns out it's karaoke night. Why don't we give it a go?'

Gabby stared at him. 'Uh-uh. No way.'

'Why not?'

She waited as he ordered their drinks and accepted her gin and tonic with perfunctory thanks as they found a tiny unoccupied table. 'Well, for a start, I can't sing.'

'Yes, you can. I heard you in the shower this morning and you sounded fine.'

'That is completely different. I will *not* stand up there and make an idiot of myself.'

'So there isn't even a tiny bit of you that wants to do it?'

'There is a tiny bit of me that wishes I was the sort of person who wants to do it, but I'm not. End of.'

'We could do it together.'

'Is this why you brought me here?'

'Yes. I even brought this to help you.' He showed her the herbal anxiety remedy he'd picked up on their way out. 'Obviously you don't have to do it if you don't want to. But I think you do. Maybe years ago you didn't just suppress grief and anger… Maybe you supressed a bit of the real you, as well.'

Her forehead creased in a frown. 'And maybe that bit is so buried it can't be retrieved. Because I really can't do this.'

'What's holding you back?'

'Fear of making a fool of myself—fear of being watched, noticed, the centre of attention.'

'But if you do it—face that fear—you'll feel good.'

'Possibly...' The admission was quiet and wrenched out of her.

'Then let's do it. After all it's only five minutes of your life. In five minutes it will be over and we can leave the pub, never to return.'

'OK. Sign me up.'

The words were blurted out, and she looked as if she regretted them instantly, but he was out of his seat before she could recant.

They waited, and listened to the two people before them. He watched as she twisted her hands together, ran her finger through a splash of water on the table to make a pattern, picked her drink up and put it back down again untouched...

'This is nuts. Why can those people just stand up and sing and I can't?'

'You can.' He stood up. 'Come on. We're up next.'

It was only as he ascended the stage that it occurred to him that he hadn't thought this through. He was going to have to read lyrics on a flickering screen from the stage, which in essence made this on a par with public speaking. It also meant it would be harder for him to help Gabby. A co-singer who couldn't read was hardly ideal.

He muttered a curse under his breath.

'What's wrong?'

'Nothing.'

Gabby looked white-faced with anxiety as it was, and he reached out for her hand, tried not to wince as she squeezed it. Somehow he'd have to wing it—hope he knew enough of the lyrics to manage.

The music started and Zander gave himself up to the whole experience—after all this *wasn't* public speaking. It didn't matter if he tanked. But the words on the flickering screen were hard to decipher, and eventually he resorted to *la-la-la* in place of the words.

Gabby had remained silent, but as she realised his predicament she turned, glanced at him, squeezed his hand even tighter, then turned back towards the audience and began to sing. Softly at first, almost as if she were trying to prompt him, and then her volume increased—and *then* her foot started to tap to the rhythm and she began to belt it out!

At the final note the audience clapped and they descended from the stage, making way for the next singers. Gabby turned to look up at him.

'I did it,' she said quietly, almost as if she couldn't believe it.

'You did.'

'Thank you, Zander. For putting yourself through that for me.' And, standing on tiptoe, she brushed her lips against his.

'You're welcome. Now, let's head home for that fish pie.'

She smiled. 'And after dinner I'll show you how grateful I am.' She wiggled her eyebrows. 'Maybe shed a few more inhibitions.'

'Now, *there's* a plan I like the sound of.'

CHAPTER TWELVE

Six weeks later

GABBY SMILED AT her grandmother, making her usual surreptitious check on how well she looked.

But today Lucille returned her scrutiny with interest. 'You look peaky,' she said. 'Is everything all right?'

'Of course. I've just been busy at work and...' *Busy with Zander, stacking up a whole pile of treasure trove memories...*

'Busy with Zander?'

Sometimes she wondered if her grandmother could read her mind. 'Yes.'

'How are you feeling about the wedding?'

Gabby knew how she *should* feel: relieved. Relieved because the wedding would mark the end of an interlude she knew couldn't continue. Already the lines had been blurred too much. The fun fling was no longer a charade, but it was still a temporary job with an end date. That date had almost arrived and it was better this way—to end on a high note before the inevitable fizzle-out factored in.

But now she needed to answer Lucille's question. 'Nervous. But relieved that the charade is coming to an end.'

Lucille raised a delicately arched brow and her blue eyes clouded with sudden worry. 'You're sure that the charade is still a charade?' she asked, her voice gentle.

'Of course. Zander will pay me the final instalment after the wedding and that will be that.'

The idea caused her more than a touch of discomfort. A part of her wanted to refuse to accept it; another part knew she couldn't. Not when it was her grandmother's well-being at stake. Plus the money grounded her, made her remember that it was a job.

Her grandmother poured the tea, a lapsang souchong blend, into delicate blue-and-white china cups and Gabby reached out to accept hers. She looked into the light brown depths and suddenly her stomach gave a small lurch. Frowning, she put the cup down. This was her favourite tea—a smell and taste she associated with her grandmother and long, happy chats. But now it smelt...*wrong*. And her tummy definitely told her not to imbibe.

'You do look peaky. A bit pale and—'

'Excuse me, Gran.' Gabby bolted for the bathroom, sat on the loo seat and fought the nausea. She looked across at the gilt-enamelled mirror— she did look peaky. Pasty, even. With a very unattractive green tinge to her pallor. *Nice*.

Touching her tummy, she thought back over what she'd eaten in the past day—nothing that would cause this.

A small strand of an idea began to niggle at the edges of her brain. A shadow of doubt wriggled and writhed as she did some frantic calculations. *Not possible*. She hadn't had a period for a while, but she was on the pill so she could not be pregnant—the possibility was not worthy of any thought. She'd assumed it was simply due to her normal life being tilted on its axis.

No period.

Feeling sick.

Coincidence.

Yet the doubt persisted through the ensuing conversation with her grandmother, through the rest of the day, and through the supermarket trip where the jars of pickled eggs seemed to call to her.

For God's sake.

Pausing in the pharmacy aisle, she picked out a pregnancy-testing kit.

Zander stood outside the Roman Baths, one of the city's most enduring historical spots, where Gemma and Alessio's wedding ceremony and reception were to take place, and reminded himself that today was a happy day. A day when his sister would wed his best friend.

But it was also the day that marked the end of his fling with Gabby. They'd decided to enjoy it and then stay at her place for their final night together.

Although... A stray thought entered his head—a thought that kept wriggling its insidious way past logic and common sense. Did it *have* to end today? Yes, the job had ended...but could they extend the fling? Prolong their time together for real?

Bad idea.

Gabby wanted love, marriage, Mr Right, a family—and God knew she deserved that chance. *He* couldn't offer her any of that.

The limousine pulled up and he stepped forward to open the door. Gabby climbed out—literally stopping him in his tracks.

'Wow. *Wow.* Just…wow.' The dress—a miasma of silver and white, a tapestry of lines that accentuated her slender shape—fell to the pavement in a swirl of elegance. Her chestnut hair was swept up in what he suspected was a deceptively simple chignon, her hazel eyes enormous in a delicately made-up face. 'And wow again.'

Her generous lips, enhanced by a deep red-brown colour, turned up in a smile. 'Right back at you,' she said. 'James Bond, eat your heart out.'

Her tone was light, but he frowned, suddenly sure that something was off. Was she a little pale? 'Are you nervous?'

Another smile, and yet it didn't reach her eyes, and it was accompanied by a small, almost hard laugh.

'Nope. The attention will be on Gemma and Alessio. Plus half the guest list are super famous, so I'll be able to fly under the radar.'

He studied her expression, saw that the words were sincere, but sensed that the idea of a celebrity bash wasn't the issue here. Which was odd in itself. What was bothering her? The fact that this day marked the end of their interlude? Did Gabby want to prolong their time together, too? If so, was that good or bad?

The questions tumbled around his brain.

'We'd better go in,' she said. 'You've got your best-man duties to attend to. I'll be fine with your family.' As they entered, she looked around. 'This is beautiful.'

Now he knew something was wrong—because this was way more than 'beautiful'. The Roman Baths were exquisite, magical with ambience, the stone walls and arches imbued with history. Guests milled around the edges of the deep blue rectangle of water that twinkled in the torchlight that cast a golden mist on the ancient surroundings. Yet Gabby's words sounded mechanical, flat—utterly unlike her usual self. And where were the facts, the research, the historical information?

But before he could respond, his family surged forward and the moment was lost. He and Gabby hugged everyone, and then he needed to go and help usher in guests with Alessio, who radiated happiness and joy.

'This beats anything! It's better than racing,

better than winning, better than being on the podium spraying champagne.'

'I'm glad for you—but you make damn sure you look after my sister, OK?'

'I will.' Alessio's tone was überserious now. 'I mean it, Zander. I promise. I'll be there for Gemma for the rest of our lives.'

The words twisted something in him, reminding him that once *he'd* believed that and been wrong. He hadn't been able to sustain love, hadn't been strong enough to figure out a way forward.

Then music struck up. The orchestra's notes hung in the air with a haunting beauty as Gemma walked forward on Frank Grosvenor's arm and all the guests fell silent. As he listened to Alessio and Gemma enunciate their vows, Zander hoped with all his heart that it would work out, that they could achieve what he hadn't been able to.

Once they had been declared husband and wife, and with the help of the ushers, Zander encouraged the guests up to the terrace, where waiters circled with drinks prior to the sit-down meal to be held in the Georgian grandeur of the Pump Room.

Then he moved across to where Gabby stood

in the shadows, a glass of orange juice in her hand, staring into space.

'Hey. Are you OK?'

'I'm fine.'

'Well, you don't look it.' A slight sheen of moisture beaded her brow, and her skin seemed to have taken on a greenish tinge. 'You look like you need to sit down.'

'I said I'm fine.'

But she swayed, and he reached out to steady her, taking the glass from her hand and stepping forward to shield her from prying eyes. 'Are you going to be sick?'

'No… Oh, God. I don't know. Probably not… but maybe. I'll head to the bathroom.'

'I'll come with you.' His hand on her back, they wended their way through the guests to the restaurant, where the staff were scurrying in a hive of activity.

Gabby headed at speed towards the bathroom and Zander waited, aware of a tightness across his chest, an elusive feeling that he was missing something important.

When Gabby emerged she looked marginally better. 'I'm OK. I wasn't sick. Usually if I just sit down for a bit I can will it away.'

'"Usually"?'

There was a beat and then another. 'I meant whenever I feel nauseous...ever since I was a child. I'm fine now.' But her hazel eyes skittered away.

'OK.' Again there was that sense he was out of the loop. And now he went with his instinct. 'If you say so. But I don't believe you. I know something is wrong and I think you should tell me.'

'Stop...'

The word was too low, too urgent, and now real panic took hold of him. 'Tell me. Are you ill?' *Shades of Claudia.* He took her hands in his, shocked at how cold her fingers were. '*Tell* me. I'll sort it out.'

She gave a small half laugh. 'I don't think you can sort this out, Zander. Not even you.'

'Then I'll help. Tell me what it is.'

'I... I'm sorry, Zander. This isn't the time or the place, but...' Gently she took her hand from his. 'I'm pregnant.'

'Pregnant?'

The word echoed, reverberated up to the lofty grandeur of the ceiling, off the iconic Georgian chandelier and flew, *ping-ping-ping*, from one fluted pillar to the next. It caused a sonic boom that vortexed around him, filled with the one word on repeat.

Pregnant.

It resounded in a sonorous toll.

Pregnant.

The meaning of the word sought entry to a brain desperate to block it out. Eventually he forced his vocal cords into action and looked down at Gabby, sitting on an elegant dining chair, surrounded by crystal and silver and pristine white napkins.

'But you can't be.'

He recognised the stupidity of the words even as he uttered them. Gabby wouldn't lie and she wouldn't make it up. Had Julia been right—had this all been an elaborate set-up? His own folly dawned on him. He'd accepted that she was on the pill, hadn't given any other protection a thought. Yet he couldn't believe he'd got it so wrong—anyway, she looked as shell-shocked as him.

'Well, I am. I told you the truth in Sintra. I am on the pill. It turns out that it's to do with that herbal remedy I was taking for anxiety—apparently in a low number of cases it can counteract the pill. It does say so in the small print. Ironic, really. All my research, all my planning, and I didn't read the small print.'

Zander wished he could think, but his brain felt as if it was encased in a gluey mix of sludge, each thought coming in slow motion. As she spoke, he had backed away from her and was now a foot away from the table. He recognised the stricken look in her eyes, looked away, caught a glimpse of his expression in an ornate gilded mirror. Horror had redrawn his features into a caricature of repudiation.

Too many emotions swirled inside him—along with the memory of Claudia, who had wanted a family. It had been Zander who had insisted on caution, on waiting. Now her voice echoed in his brain.

'Zan. I think we should go for it. I know we're young, but that's OK. Let's start a family—not a business.'

And he'd resisted, prevaricated, knowing his own dream would be given up, would flicker out before ever catching light. Then illness had struck and all their energy had been for the fight and then acceptance. Claudia hadn't ever got to hold a baby in her arms...and now Gabby would.

Gabby was carrying *his* baby.

The whole idea jarred in his brain and he felt something inside him shattering—illusions, plans, certainties. All were coated with a layer of guilt. It was all he could do to remain still, not to run from the room with its Regency splendour.

Gabby rose to her feet. 'I'm sorry. I didn't want to tell you now—not like this...not at the wedding. I know this isn't what you want.'

Her hand went to her tummy, lay flat over it almost as if she were protecting the baby from his reaction, from his words. The gesture dispersed the fog, cut through the sludge. None of this was the baby's fault. Zander's guilt and emotion, his past behaviours, failures and fears, had nothing to do with the miraculous being growing in Gabby's womb.

'Don't apologise. Of course you had to tell me. Why didn't you tell me before?'

'Because I didn't know how, and it didn't seem fair before the wedding. But...now you know. We're having a baby.'

Now he knew.

Images streamed through his brain. A baby with chestnut hair like Gabby's...another with dark blonde hair like his, hazel eyes...blue, grey...so many permutations and possibilities.

Then panic broke in, short-circuited the connection and dispersed the images. How could he be a dad? He wasn't a family man; he was a businessman. And in his case the two were mutually exclusive. *But that wasn't this baby's fault.*

He had to focus. This was his baby. That was the precious being he needed to think of now. Not himself. Right now the two most important people on the planet were Gabby and the baby.

'Now I know,' he repeated.

'Know what?'

A voice behind them. Zander spun round to see Julia walking towards them, a vision in a red-and-black gown.

'Know that we need to be on wedding duty,' he improvised quickly.

'Yes, you do. It's time to move the guests in here for dinner. I came in to double-check the seating plan.'

She moved back to the entrance and Zander took Gabby's hand as she rose. 'We need to talk.'

Gabby nodded. 'But not now.'

'And, Gabs? Everything will be all right.'

Right now he wasn't sure how—all he knew was that somehow he had to make it so. Even if he had no idea how. Even if the idea of fatherhood was making his skin clammy with sheer, unadulterated terror.

Gabby walked by Zander's side back to the gaiety and hum of chatter and laughter, the pop of champagne corks, the vibe of celebration, and tried to focus on the part she was here to play. She was no longer sure what that even was—everything was surreal as her emotions corkscrewed.

Sharing the news had brought a modicum of relief along with a surge of misery. Saying the words had made it real, but the initial horror on Zander's face and his gesture of repudiation had hurt, even though she understood it.

He'd been taken by surprise. But he'd recovered enough to tell her everything would be 'all right'. Whatever *that* meant.

'Gabby, come over here for a photo,' she heard Gemma call out, and she walked over, pinned a smile to her face.

She looked at the Grosvenors with the sudden realisation that they were related to the baby growing inside her, and the idea sent her emotions into free fall again. But somehow she

pulled herself together, and she kept herself together over the next few hours.

She tried to appreciate the grandeur of the
Pump Room, the classical melodies played so
beautifully by the orchestra, the Georgian ban-
quet that drew gasps of awe from the guests.

Once the meal was over the guests moved into
yet another room. Music struck up again and the
bride and groom took to the floor. Gabby felt her
chest constrict as she watched, seeing the love in
Gemma's and Alessio's expressions, the protec-
tive, almost reverent way Alessio held his bride,
and she blinked back tears. What if this never
happened for her?

Then Gemma turned and gestured to her.
'Come on. Family on the floor next!'

Laura and Frank moved forward and started
to dance, their movements so attuned to each
other, the smiles on their faces only for each
other. Julia was dragged forward by Freddy and
Heidi, and soon the three of them were dancing,
laughing together.

'Zander, come on!'

Gabby realised there was no choice, and put
her hand into his proffered one. They stepped
on to the floor. His arm encircled her waist and

she felt his reaction, his small intake of breath, and knew he was realising the fact that inside her was the start of a baby. *Their* baby.

As they swayed together to the music, she allowed worry and anxiety to dissipate in the awe-inspiring knowledge that she and Zander had created the beginnings of a new life. She let him hold her close, and rested her head on the solid wall of his chest.

They stayed until the end, waved off the bride and groom, said farewell to the rest of the family, gave a hug to the sleepy children—and then they were back outside, where a chauffeur-driven car waited to take them home.

'What would you like to do?' Zander asked.

'We'd better stick to the plan. Go back to mine. But...' She hesitated. 'Would you mind sleeping on the sofa bed?' She might have no idea where they would go from here, but she knew the fun fling was definitely over. 'Tomorrow we'll talk.'

CHAPTER THIRTEEN

GABBY OPENED HER eyes and tried to orientate herself... And then slowly memory seeped back in. She was pregnant. In seven or eight months she'd be a mum. In all her dreams this was not how she'd imagined it. The plan had been to find Mr Right, get married, buy a house—provide her baby with two loving parents, security, a happy family life, siblings...

Well, that plan had gone...dispersed into wisps of illusion. Touching her tummy, she pushed away the feeling of inadequacy, of not being good enough.

'I'll figure it out, baby. I promise,' she said aloud.

And she would. Somehow. And the first step towards that was to talk to Zander.

A tantalising aroma wafted into the room and she used the bathroom, then pulled on her clothes with the realisation that she was ravenous.

Two minutes later she entered her lounge and

crossed the room to the kitchenette, seeing that Zander had already packed away the sofa bed in the lounge and had set up the circular fold-away table. A vase of flowers was in the middle, surrounded by slate place mats, knives, forks, chocolate spread, fresh lemons... The air was permeated with the smell of bacon sizzling.

Zander stood at the kitchen counter that separated the lounge and kitchen areas, stirring a bowl of batter. 'Pancakes,' he announced. He glanced up at her, then back down at the bowl, a faint flush on his cheeks. 'My dad used to make pancakes every Sunday morning. I figured we could start the tradition early—the baby eats what you eat, right?"

The words brought a sudden sting of tears to her eyes but she blinked them away. 'Sounds perfect. I'll put the kettle on.'

Fifteen minutes later they sat down, a mound of pancakes between them, and Gabby dug in, relieved that the nausea seemed to have been flummoxed by the notion of pancakes. Maybe the baby liked them? The idea made her smile. Or maybe the baby liked the fact this was his or her first family meal.

Whoa—that idea wiped the smile from her lips.

It was a stark reminder of what she'd wanted for her children—the real thing, a happy family...

She pushed her empty plate away. 'So...' she said.

'So,' he answered.

He looked a different man today, no longer shocked, no longer horrified. Instead his expression indicated a man in control of his emotions.

'First, I apologise for my initial reaction yesterday—you took me by surprise and I was utterly shocked.'

'I appreciate the apology, but I saw your face when I told you—that was more than shock or surprise. That was horror. I know you don't want children, and I don't want my baby to feel unwanted or unloved. I can't bear that thought.' She truly couldn't. A tear quivered on the edge of her eyelash. 'I *was* that baby—the unwanted one. The unwanted child. That will *not* happen to this baby. Not for a second. Not on my watch.'

His blue-grey eyes didn't leave hers as he reached out to cover her hand with his own. 'This baby won't be unwanted or unloved, and I swear to you that I regret my reaction. It wasn't horror. It was...' He hesitated. 'I don't know what it was. Disbelief, guilt, panic. You see, Claudia wanted to start a family. I was the one who held back—partly because I knew once we had a baby I would never be able to chase my dreams. Then she fell ill…never had a chance to be a mum.'

Oh, God. His reaction made sense now. The idea of fatherhood must seem almost like a betrayal of Claudia—an extra lash of the guilt he already felt.

'It's not your fault.'

But his set expression told her he thought it was.

'You didn't know Claudia would die so tragically young. You thought you had plenty of time. Maybe you weren't ready to be a parent so young, even if Claudia was. That is not a sin. Maybe in the end you'd have found a compromise between family and business—the tragedy is that you'll never have a chance to find out.'

'I know that logically, but if I had reacted differently, if I'd been a different person, maybe she could have held her baby in her arms. But, whatever happened with Claudia and I, this baby will *not* bear the brunt of the past. You're right—I didn't plan to have children, but now I want to be the best father I can.'

'I want to be the best mother I can.'

'And I know a way for us to do just that.'

'I'm all ears.' Lord knew she'd welcome a plan of action.

He inhaled deeply, exhaled, sipped his coffee and then said, 'I think we should get married.'

Gabby froze. 'Come again? You think we should *what*?' Frantically her brain tried to come up with words that rhymed with *married*. *Tarried... Carried...*

'Get married.'

'You and me?'

'Yes.' His tone held exaggerated patience. 'Seeing as *you* are pregnant with *my* baby—yes. You and me.' His gaze didn't leave hers; his blue-grey eyes were utterly serious. 'I know I'm not Mr Right, but it is the right thing to do.'

'But you don't want to get married. You don't want any sort of relationship.'

'I *didn't* want either of those things, but now the situation has changed. I didn't plan on being a father, but now that it's happening I want to do the best I can, and that means being there for my child.'

Gabby picked up her orange juice, put it down again, tried to work out what to say, what to do. Eventually she shook her head. 'No. I appreciate that you want to do your duty, do the "right" thing, but I told you—I never want this baby to feel it's a burden or a duty. You can be a good father without us getting married.'

'I believe I will be a better one if we are. I am doing this because I want to. For the baby. I know I don't have to. I accept that it is perfectly OK nowadays to parent separately. But that isn't what I want. I want to be there under the same roof, be there for the firsts, be there for meals, holidays, be there when he or she needs me. We'd be a *family*.'

Under the same roof... A family... The words resonated within her, made a sense of rightness course through her veins. Their baby would grow up with one proper home, the security of not having to move from house to house. But...

'Yes, we'd be a family, but our marriage wouldn't be—'

'It wouldn't be how you want your marriage to be. I know that. It would be different—based on liking and respect and physical compatibility.' His gaze skittered from hers for a moment. 'Not love. I understand that's second-best for you, that you hoped for a happy-ever-after with Mr Right, but you said it yourself—Mr Right may never turn up. I think we could be happy—or certainly not *un*happy. You also said you wouldn't have children until you could offer them two loving parents and security. We can give our baby both those things. Together.'

Gabby's mind reeled. Thoughts ravelled and unravelled as she tried to think, to consider the ramifications of his suggestion. Because whatever she'd expected his reaction to be it wasn't this. Marriage was not what he wanted, and a marriage without love was not what *she* wanted—and yet he was right; the baby changed everything. All she'd wanted was for her mother to be willing to change her lifestyle for her. Zander had just shown that he was willing to do that for his child. Surely she was, too?

If they got married, their baby would have one home, wouldn't have to move from her home to Zander's in a constant cycle of change. It would have a family—Zander's parents, his sisters—he'd have cousins. And… A stray thought crept in… And so would Gabby. Sisters-in-law who might become friends, parents-in-law…

Gabby closed her eyes, contemplated all those solid tangible reasons for marriage. But… 'How would it work? In real life, I mean. Where would we live? What about my job?'

There was so much to think about. She loved her flat, but it wasn't big enough for a baby. She loved her job, but did she want to keep working? If she didn't keep working how would she support the baby? She wouldn't live off Zander. So that answered that. But then...

'Whoa, Gabby. *Stop.*'

Looking down, she realised she'd helped herself to the last remaining pancake and had been spooning sugar on to it in a continual stream.

'I know this is a lot to think about but we'll work it out. Do you want to live in Bath? Do you want to keep working?' he asked.

'Yes. And yes. I need to stay near Gran and I would like to stay on at least part-time.'

'Then we'll live in Bath.'

'But you'd have to commute.'

Zander's work ethos: another reason in favour of marriage. Zander's work was his life; if his child lived under his roof it would maximise their relationship potential.

'It's only an hour and a half by train. Or I could get a driver...work in the car. That would be compensated for by all the other advantages. We'd be near my family, your job, your gran.'

'You'd do that?''

'Sure. It truly doesn't matter to me. A house is a house.'

'No. A house is a *home*—I want my child to have a home. *I* need a home.'

'Of course. I'll leave all that to you.'

The words triggered a sense of sadness, a reminder of the terms of this marriage—in her dreams of Mr Right they'd picked furniture together, debated every purchase, painted walls, chosen wallpaper for the nursery. This would be another fake relationship with Zander, but this time it would have no end date.

As if he'd picked up the motes of her dissolved dreams in the air he frowned, reached out and gently touched her cheek. 'We don't have to get married. I won't try to bulldoze you into it. I get that you may want to hold out for Mr Right, and I don't want to make you give up a dream if you'll regret it for the rest of your life. But if we do get married I will need an assurance that you won't still be on the lookout.'

Outrage jolted into a welcome spark of anger. 'I wouldn't do that. If I marry you, Zander, I'll honour my vows and my commitment—and I'll expect you to do the same.'

Unlike Miles and Steve. Another advantage to this type of marriage: it wouldn't turn her into an insecure, needy nutcase. There would be rules, a maintenance manual she would understand because she would help write it.

'I would. That's the point I'm making. This marriage can only work if we're both happy with its parameters and our expectations. There is no point getting married for the sake of our child if what he or she witnesses is anger or misery. And...' He gave a rueful shrug. 'And I don't want you to be angry or unhappy.'

'Ditto.'

'I truly believe we can make this work. Arranged marriages have worked throughout the centuries. Unions based on something other than love.' He leant back as if to give her space. 'So what do you think?'

What did she *think*? This was her chance to give her baby everything she'd ever wanted as a child. In truth she wouldn't have cared if her parents had loved each other or not as long as they had seemed happy; she had wanted love, a family life, a home and security. Her child would have all those things if she married Zander. So really it was a no-brainer. She had to try or she'd always regret it.

She just had to ignore that voice in her head that still argued...

'I think we should do it. So I suppose the next step is to share the news.'

'Agreed. I'll tell my family.'

'And I'll tell Gran.'

The next day
Bath, Lucille's house

Telling her gran had been much harder than Gabby had anticipated. At first Lucille had been genuinely thrilled about the baby, and definitely happy that Zander wanted to be part of the baby's life, but then Gabby had gone on. 'And we've decided to get married!'

For reasons she couldn't quite understand, her voice had come out overbright, high and squeaky, and her arms had, of their own volition, lifted to cross her chest.

'Why?'

There was no judgement in Lucille's voice, but worry clouded the blue eyes that just seconds ago had been bright with joy.

'Because we feel it's the best thing for the baby. He or she will have both parents under one roof, won't have to move from house to house and will have a proper family life. It will work around Zander's work ethos, maximise his time with the baby, and I'll be giving the baby a family. If anything happens to me, he'll have *them*. The Grosvenors.' She came to a stop, searched her gran's face for approval that wasn't there. 'I don't have a choice.'

'There is *always* a choice.'

'Then I believe this is the right one. This baby deserves to have what you and Gramps gave me. A family—that is what is most important.'

'But *you* are important, too.'

'I know that. And if I loathed Zander, of course I wouldn't do this. But we like each other, we have mutual respect and he is a good man. I'll have a good life.'

'A *good* life—but will it be the best life you can have? It's your life. You only get one.'

'Yes. But I have to do what's best for my child—that is paramount.'

Her grandmother looked troubled. 'Of course your child comes first. But I don't think it's necessary to sacrifice your life.'

'It's hardly a sacrifice.'

Lucille sipped her tea. 'But it *is*. You are twenty-nine years old and you and Zander are making a decision to give up on love, never to have a marriage like I had with Gramps.'

'But I may *never* meet my Mr Right.'

'This way you definitely won't. Instead you will be making a commitment to a loveless marriage—in sickness and in health, for better and for worse.'

The words and their solemnity rang around the room, and Gabby scrabbled to scoop up the seed of doubt before it could take root.

'What if your child *knows* you got married only for him or her?' Lucille continued. 'That you would have preferred not to? That's a burden for a child. I always worried when you were young that you thought your grandfather and I took you out of duty.'

Gabby closed her eyes. She *had* thought that, and it had been a horrible feeling—a precursor to guilt and self-reproach.

'We didn't. We took you because we loved you. Our biggest fear was that we wouldn't be allowed to keep you.'

'That was my biggest fear, too. That's why I

want my child to have absolute security. I don't want him or her to move from home to home. That's worth the trade-off to me. I truly believe this is the right thing to do.'

Lucille hesitated, topped up her cup of tea. 'Gabby. Are you sure this is only about the baby?'

'What do you mean?'

'You and Zander have spent a lot of time together, and from all you've told me you've enjoyed that time—are you *sure* that you don't have stronger feelings for him?'

Gabby barely even waited for her gran to finish the sentence. 'I am absolutely sure. Zander is a good man, Gran, but he isn't my Mr Right.'

Too successful, too good-looking, too overwhelming. She wouldn't *want* to love him—she sensed that that way lay a path to doom, a return to neediness and insecurity.

'Then I will support your choice, even if I don't agree with it. And I will be the best great-grandmother ever.'

'I know you will, Gran.'

Bath, the Grosvenor home

Telling his family had been tough, but once they had established that he was planning on being part of the baby's life they did seem genuinely happy at the idea of an addition to the family.

But then he said, 'Actually, Gabby and I are getting married.'

Silence greeted the announcement—a silence so profound that annoyance surfaced, came out in his scowl.

'Don't all fall over at once congratulating me.'

His parents and Julia exchanged a quick glance, and as if by tacit consent his mum spoke. 'The thing is, Zander, you haven't mentioned the word *love.*'

Damn right, he hadn't. The word filled him with panic. Love would bring this marriage to its knees—he couldn't sustain it and didn't want to contemplate it. But the word also inspired guilt, because Gabby *did* want love and he couldn't give it to her.

'Gabby and I want what is best for the baby, and we like each other… We get on. There is no reason why it shouldn't work.'

'There are at least a dozen reasons I can think of,' Julia interjected. 'God knows, Zander, I think a child should have a father…' Her voice was touched with a seldom-acknowledged sadness; her husband had decided the whole family gig was too much for him and absconded over the horizon. 'But you can have joint custody—you will still be part of its life.'

'Not in the same way.' Zander turned to his parents. 'Tell me *you* approve.'

Laura and Frank exchanged looks. They had one of those telepathic methods of communication that seemed to be a product of all their years together.

Laura spoke. 'Darling, we will support whatever you choose to do, but I don't think I do approve. I want you to marry for love.'

'Dad?'

'I always hoped you'd find love again, Zander. I understand why you're doing this, but I believe you and Gabby can and will be fantastic parents whether you get married or not. We will welcome both Gabby and the baby into our family, regardless of your marital status.'

Zander looked around the table, then rose to his feet. It was time to go. In this instance his family was wrong. It was as simple as that.

'I love you all, but I want to be there for my baby as much as possible—and that means marriage.'

A few days later

Gabby surveyed her breakfast without appetite or enthusiasm and told herself that sugar-free muesli was good for the baby, who could not, after all, survive on pickled eggs alone. And she needed to hurry up. Zander would be here at any minute to take her on a day out—though he'd declined to say any more than that. Told her it was a surprise.

She spooned up the last unappetising mouthful and patted her tummy. 'Maybe there will be pickled eggs later, baby.'

As she finished speaking the doorbell heralded Zander's arrival. Gabby opened the door and her tummy looped the loop—was she really going to marry a man who did this to her?

Zander smiled at her. 'Ready to go?'

Gabby grabbed a denim jacket, tugged it over her T-shirt and jeans. 'I am now.'

Once in the passenger seat of his car, she turned to him. 'So where are we going?'

'I told you—it's a surprise.' He glanced at her before turning the ignition, and concern lit his blue-grey eyes. 'It's an hour till we get to our first port of call, so if you want to nap go ahead.'

She *was* tired. As soon as she went to bed

each night questions marched behind her eyelids, along with doubts and worry as to whether she was doing the right thing for the baby. Yet now, when she closed her eyes, lulled by the movement of the car and his presence, she slept, opening her eyes only when the car came to a stop.

'Where are we?'

'A helipad. We're flying by helicopter to Cornwall and we're going to Tintagel Castle. I did some research and the flight is completely safe for the baby. But if you feel worried, obviously I'll change the plan.'

Helicopter. It occurred to Gabby that for Zander taking a helicopter was akin to hopping in a taxi. The realisation was a reminder of just how wealthy he was, and for a moment discomfort tugged at her chest.

She blinked to dispel the unease. Zander had planned this, and it would be churlish not to simply appreciate it. 'Let's go!'

Twenty minutes later they approached the craft and she gazed at it in surreal fascination. 'I've never seen one close up.'

'I'll climb in first and then help you. You need to use the footplates, and then there's a big step up to get in.'

Once inside she settled back, and soon the whir of the blades made conversation impossible.

The eventual take-off was completely different to that of a plane.

'It's as if we've just lifted and floated upwards,' she said.

Once they were airborne the noise abated a bit and she looked down over London, watching as it became smaller and smaller, the familiar landmarks looking like little toy miniatures.

'So why Tintagel?' she asked.

'I figured I owe you a castle after Sintra, and I thought it would be good to spend a day together away from familiar haunts. Give us a chance to centre ourselves. It's been a pretty momentous few days.'

The rest of the journey was spent watching the landscape. The aerial perspective of rich swirls of brown and green dotted with farm buildings, grey blocks of towns and cities, caught her breath with its sheer variety. Then finally there was the intense sweep of the sea that indicated they were nearly at their destination, a prelude to the helicopter's descent.

As they alighted from the craft, the Cornish breeze combined with the whir of the helicopter blades to lift her hair in a wild tangle and puff out her clothes so she resembled a fairground mirror reflection.

Once en route in the hired car, Gabby gave herself up to the sheer pleasure of watching the beauty of the Cornish countryside flash past. The fields were full of summer—the golden swish of corn, the deep brown loam of tilled earth—and stacked hay dotted the horizon. The drone of a tractor through the open window mixed with the buzz of insects, whilst cows and sheep watched their journey with placid interest. They passed a farmhouse, and then the green changed shade as the landscape turned to scrubland and then back again.

At the end of a half-hour journey Tintagel came into view, the ruined castle a craggy, impressive feature that loomed over the headland to the sea.

'Tintagel is where King Arthur is said to have been conceived—you can't get much more magical than that,' she said.

'Then let's go.'

As they walked from the car park Gabby had an urge to take his hand, but held back, unsure as to the etiquette. Somehow, to hold hands now they were getting married seemed to imply a level of intimacy unsuitable in an arranged union. Instead she allowed herself to enjoy the warmth of his presence, to appreciate the thought that had gone into this trip.

The short walk to the ticket office was achieved in companionable silence and then they began the trek to the castle ruins, pausing as they looked across a wooden bridge and up…and up…at the steep ascent.

Zander frowned. 'I should have researched this better. I got hooked on historical splendour and magical legends. I'm not sure you should climb this.'

Gabby considered for a moment. 'The doctor said I'd be fine with exercise.'

'Hmm… Hang on. I'm going to call Julia for advice.' Minutes later Zander dropped the phone in his pocket. 'Right, Julia said she went rock climbing in her first trimester with Heidi and was fine. Her advice is to try it, but to turn back if there is any problem, however small, and to take it slowly.'

'Yes, sir!'

His concern made her feel…cared for. *Alert! Alert!* His care was, as it should be, for the *baby.*

As they walked across the bridge he stayed close to her. Every so often he reached out as if to steady her, and she smiled up at him as they paused, arm in arm, and looked over the rail at a sea that was a clear sun-sparkled turquoise.

He pointed downward. 'Merlin's cave.'

'I can almost imagine a dragon swooping down to visit him.'

Then came the stairs and, as instructed, she took them slowly, very aware of his focus, of the heat of his gaze as he made sure she was all right, his hand on the small of her back to help her.

And then they reached the top and she gasped in sheer awe. The ruins themselves were darkly atmospheric, though the arched doorway and slit windows were all that remained of the great hall. Low stone walls marked where houses, kilns and a chapel would once have teemed with people and medieval life.

But it was the view that literally caught at her newly recovered breath. The headlands were a myriad of jutting rocks, in shades of green, brown and terracotta. And way below the sea crashed with all the force and power of nature against the rocks.

'It's a place where your imagination can swoop and soar… You can almost *taste* history.'

Zander's eyes rested on her face. 'I've brought something perhaps a little more sustaining if you want to picnic up here. I even brought pickled eggs.'

'That sounds wonderful!'

Soon enough he had unpacked a hamper bearing the logo of a famous London store and Gabby got down to the serious business of eating for two. Mini quiches, game pie, pâté and crackers, and, of course, the pickled eggs were all washed down with sparkling elderflower pressé.

Eventually she sat back, replete. 'Thank you. That was delicious and it has fortified me for the trek back down!'

'Before we do that… I thought it would be a good time to give you this.' Reaching into his pocket, he pulled out a small box, snapped the lid up and handed it to her.

A jolt of emotion shot through her as she saw the glint and sparkle of the ring embedded in velvet—a beautiful mix of an ice-white diamond and deep blue lapis lazuli set in white gold.

'If you don't like it we can change it.'

'No! It's stunning.'

Carefully she took it out, looked at it for a long moment. Suddenly the whole ambience of the day shifted, and as if in response a cloud moved across the sun for an instant.

Don't overthink it, Gabs.

Quickly now, she slipped it on to her ring finger—he didn't offer to do it and in truth it wouldn't have felt right if he had. Too much like a parody. After all, this ring was not an indicator of love, merely an intention of commitment without it. A prop rather than a symbol.

Holding her hand up, she watched as the newly reappeared sun sparkled in the stones' facets, causing motes of light to dance in the air. Yet for some reason her finger felt weighted.

'The central stone is a diamond, obviously, and the blue stones are lapis lazuli—the colour reminded me of the sea and Sintra, and the jeweller said they represent friendship.'

Now sadness truly prodded her—a definite sense of *This is not how it's meant to be.* Yes, the ring was beautiful, the idea brilliant, but the most important component was missing.

Stop it, Gabby.

This was not the time to be whiny or act the ingrate—Zander had gone to a huge effort and she should appreciate it. Because in their marriage friendship, not love, would be the cornerstone. Love for their child was the bedrock.

'It's perfect,' she said. 'And thank you for making an occasion of it.'

'I thought it was important. After all, one day our child will ask us where we got engaged. My sisters were always asking Mum and Dad to tell their engagement story.'

'I used to love hearing Gran and Gramps's, as well. Gramps hired a tandem and asked Gran to ride through life with him. He said that he'd pedal harder when she needed to rest and that they'd always balance each other out on their journey through life together.' As always, the story brought a smile to her lips, though the memory was touched now by the sadness of missing him. 'What was your parents' story?'

Zander smiled in reminiscence. 'I told you Dad's an electrician? He rigged up loads and loads of fairy lights in their local park, hired a violinist and told her she was the light of his life. And she really is—his face still lights up when she comes into a room and vice versa.'

'And what about you and Claudia?' Gabby

didn't know why she'd asked that—perhaps because that was what a *friend* would ask.

The thought tasted bitter on her tongue and she picked up her glass and gulped at a swig of elderflower.

Zander hesitated. 'I was only eighteen and I went for the romantic cliché. I saved up, took her out for an expensive meal, gave her a red rose and a ring. All the other diners clapped when she said yes.'

She could see it now—the earnest youth he had been, at a time of life when he had still been struggling to come to terms with and conquer his dyslexia and all that had come with it. His dark blonde hair had probably been longer than it was now, flopping forward over one eye, and he would have been dressed up in a suit. Claudia, young and beautiful, would have been alight with the glow of optimism, hope and love.

His parents, her grandparents... Their proposal stories had been full of love—a foretaste of their hopes and dreams of going through life together with love to guide their movements. Whereas this...this was kind and thoughtful and...*all wrong*.

She wanted Zander to be down on one knee,

slipping the ring on her finger for real. Because he loved her, not because it would make a good story for their child. She wanted love, not friendship, because she loved him and, dammit, she wanted this to be *real*.

Oh, hell. The drink suddenly tasted too sickly-sweet, cloying on her tongue. She loved him. She *loved* him. She loved Zander. Her Mr Wrong. *What to do? What to do?*

'Gabby? What's the matter?'

Panic, horror, terror—all fused into an icy coldness, enabling hard logic to overcome emotion. Whatever she did, she could not let him suspect the truth, learn of her misplaced, idiotic, unwanted love. A love he would reject just as surely as her mother had rejected her love all those years ago.

But now this marriage would be impossible. How could she hope to make it work when the rules and parameters had exploded? Even *she* couldn't live a lie, play a part for the rest of her life, day in, day out, yearning for what she couldn't have.

He mustn't know—must not suspect even the possibility that love had somehow had the temerity to take root and flourish within her for him. This wasn't his fault. None of it was.

So now she would have to play a different part—tell him the truth, but not the whole truth. Above all she had to make this work for the baby's sake. It was impossible for her simply to walk out of Zander's life, but somehow she had to figure out a way to rip this love out by its fledgling roots.

The glint of the ring was harsh now, carrying the weight of falsehood, and she tugged it off and held it out to him. 'I'm sorry, Zander. I can't do this.'

Shock etched his face, turned it white under the tan, and his body jerked backwards as an expression she couldn't interpret flashed across his blue-grey eyes. But his voice was calm when he spoke. 'Why not?'

Deep breath. *Careful, here, Gabby.*

'Because we would both be settling for second best, and that is not how I want to teach my child to live his or her life. It is not what a marriage should be. A marriage should at least start out like your parents' did, like my grandparents' did, like yours did. You don't want to get married. You told me that don't want to marry anyone, and you certainly don't want to marry me. You want to marry the mother of your child for your child's sake, and I honour that sentiment but it makes me second-best and secondary. I can't spend my life like that. I still want my shot at love with Mr Right.'

Those last words were the hardest, but she forced them out, knowing they would help her argument.

A small hope flared that Zander would step up, reach out, grab the ring and say, 'Gabby I love you. I want a marriage based on love, too,' then place the ring back on her finger as a gesture of loving commitment to her and the baby.

Her insides clenched and her heart pounded with a sheer yearning that the scenario would play out that way—that he, too, would have a eureka moment, realise that the past weeks had been more than a charade, more than just fun.

The seconds ticked on, each one full of anguish as she watched his face, saw confusion and pain. She wished so hard that he would love her back, *could* love her back. For herself.

Tick-tock. On and on.

Finally his lips opened and she braced herself.

'What about the baby?' he asked.

As hope died, crumbled to ashes, she stared down at the ring, at the lapis lazuli blinking at her in a kind of Morse code: *friendship, friendship, friendship.* That was all she could hope to have, and she would make that OK for the baby's sake. Before that, though, she needed space and time, to get her head together and bury this foolish love as in the past she had buried grief and anger. She'd learn her part and play it perfectly.

'First take the ring,' she said. 'Please.'

CHAPTER FOURTEEN

ZANDER STARED AT her outstretched palm. The ring glinted at him in all its suddenly cold hard beauty. He'd chosen it for Gabby; he didn't want it back. Staring at the blue stones, the white faceted diamond, he tried to think. But his brain had gone into shutdown mode, and the urge to sit on his hands, make her put the ring back on her finger, was paramount.

'What about the baby?' he repeated. After all, that was why they'd decided to get married. 'I thought we had agreed this was best for our child. The right thing to do.'

Now she winced, and a dark part of him was glad—because perhaps he could persuade her that marriage was the right option.

'We did.' Her voice low, torn, ragged with guilt. 'But I can't go through with it. I'm sorry.'

'I want to be part of this child's life.'

'You will be. I want that, too. Of course I do. I promise we can sit down and work out custody arrangements. I want this baby to have you and your family in his life.'

'And, like we've said, the best way to do that is if you and I and the baby are under the same roof. Instead of moving from house to house.'

Stop! The voice was a Klaxon in his head as he saw the look of pain on her face and knew his words had triggered memories of her own childhood, the packing of her suitcase...

But that had been his intention, hadn't it? Number one bastard that he was. How low was he willing to go in his belief that this marriage was right? And right for *who* anyway? Maybe it was better for the baby, but not at the cost of Gabby's happiness, her life. She deserved a shot at her Mr Right—someone able to believe in love and for ever, someone able to commit and not prioritise work over love.

Not someone like Zander, with a proved track record of failure, a lack of capacity to nurture love, to be satisfied with what he had. He was a man who revered ambition, craved success, and he would never be able to put a family first.

Yes, this marriage would suit *him*—because he wouldn't have to put Gabby first. He could have it all. So he was trying to bulldoze her into a marriage she didn't want, a life she didn't want. *No more.*

Yet as he prepared to speak, an inexplicable sense of loss tore into him. For a searing moment he imagined the life that had nearly been his—a life with Gabby, a family life, with trips to the supermarket, holidays, meals, laughter. He watched as the images of that illusory life faded and dispersed in the breeze. Because that wasn't reality. He couldn't offer her love because he knew that for him the emotion wasn't sustainable, knew that it couldn't coexist with his ambition. His plans revolved around his work, and he'd always known it wasn't possible to have a family, as well. Hadn't he?

'It's OK, Gabby,' he said, even as he knew it wasn't. It wasn't OK at all to have this dark bleakness descend on his heart. His arm felt heavy, inert, but he forced himself to reach out and take the ring. 'We'll make this work a different way.'

'How?'

'Tell the baby the truth. That we both love him or her...'

'But we don't love each other,' she broke in. 'That we're friends. And maybe two homes will be OK as long as they're both full of love and security.'

'Yes.' He forced conviction into his voice and his expression, but inside a sudden bleak disappointment washed over him—a pain he didn't fully understand. 'So what now?'

Gabby hugged her knees, stared out to sea. 'Well, there are still seven months until the baby is due. If you want to attend antenatal classes with me, of course you can, and I'll keep you posted on how the pregnancy is going. But otherwise there's no longer any need for us to see each other. No more charade, no more engagement.'

No more Gabby.

As he sat there, so near her and yet so very, very far away, the bleakness increased. It felt like a jagged tear in his chest. He had a sense that he had failed, that he had missed something crucial. They sat in silence for a long time, both looking out at the crags and cliffs, the imposing Cornish coastline and the deep blue of the sea, until finally Gabby shifted.

'We should go,' she said.

Zander nodded, told himself it was for the best. He couldn't sustain relationships, and he didn't understand compromise. He would never again risk love because he knew he couldn't nurture it. On his watch it would fray, wither and fade away.

He told himself that now he could focus on work—take his company to even greater heights without any distraction for the next seven months. And after that he would work out a balance between the baby and work without having to factor Gabby in at all. It was all for the best.

So why did his very soul feel so heavy as they trudged towards the steps he'd climbed in such anticipation?

A month later
Bath, Lucille's house

Gabby smoothed her hand over her growing bump and smiled at her grandmother. The baby seemed to have rejuvenated Lucille.

'I'll be here on this green earth for as long as I can be. Here for the baby and for you, Gabrielle,' she said.

'I hope you're here for years and years, Gran.'

Thank heaven for Lucille—her family, her rock. And a welcome distraction from thoughts of Zander.

Gabby had hoped that a month without seeing

him would at least have started a cure for love, would have stunted its growth, made it less intense. But with each passing day the sheer ache of missing him intensified until all she wanted to do was call him, just to hear his voice.

But she didn't. Her plan, such as it was, was to starve this love until eventually it would have to perish. She tried to ration even her thoughts of him—so far without noticeable success.

'Gabby?'

'Sorry, Gran. I was thinking.'

'So have I been.'

'About what?' Idly, Gabby reached out for one of the small square marzipan-topped cakes which were her current craving.

'Do you love Zander?'

The sheer unexpectedness of the question caught Gabby off guard and the cake dropped from her suddenly nerveless fingers, crashed on to her plate in a scatter of iced crumbs. 'Of course not.'

'Gabrielle. I'm an old lady, but I've known you all your life. Tell me the truth—I want to help and I know you aren't happy.'

'I *am* happy. I'm happy about the baby. A bit terrified, but mostly happy.'

'And what about Zander?' Lucille persisted. 'Gabby, you can tell me. That's what family is for.'

Gabby hesitated, and then the need to confide, to share the secret that burned within her with her gran, overcame her doubts. 'I do love him. But he doesn't know and he mustn't ever know.'

'Why not?'

'He doesn't want my love, Gran, and I can't face the humiliation of inciting his pity or compassion.' She couldn't take the rejection. 'Plus, it would make things complicated, and that's not fair on the baby. We've agreed to explain that we're friends, that we don't love each other but we both love him or her.'

Her gran frowned, her delicate skin creasing. 'But that's not true. You said you wanted to tell your child the truth, that you didn't want to live a lie by getting married. This will be living a lie, too.'

'For my child.'

'No, Gabby. It will be years before he or she is worried about the intricacies of the relationship between his parents. I don't think this is about the baby. I think it's about *you*. And, darling, I understand how scared you must be of having your love rejected again. Like your mother did. But I know that I would have told your grandfather I loved him no matter what. Because love should always be given a chance. And if Zander does reject that love I know you're strong enough to face it and move forward.'

The last words were slurred slightly and Gabby could see the forcefulness of her speech had tired her grandmother.

Quickly she poured another cup of tea, and then she covered her gran's veined hand with her own. 'Thank you. I'll think about it. I promise.'

And later, when she had gone back home, she did. She would never break a promise to her gran, so she thought about it long and hard. Replayed every word Lucille had uttered.

She closed her eyes and cringed at the idea of the pity, the compassion, the sheer awkwardness such a confession would generate. Yet Gran was right—love deserved a chance.

Gabby stared at the ceiling and made her decision, then snuggled down under her duvet and told herself it was the right thing to do.

Zander drummed his fingers on the desk and stared at his phone, willing it to ring and for it to be Gabby. Saying what? He closed his eyes. They had said everything they needed to say. Antenatal classes didn't start for weeks, and until then the baby quite simply did not need him. Neither did Gabby—and he certainly didn't need her. Though it was galling to realise how much he missed her. Somehow during the charade Gabby had got under his skin, permeated his life in ways he hadn't foreseen and didn't know how to combat.

His intercom buzzed and his PA's voice rang out. 'Your sisters are here.'

'Both of them?'

For heaven's sake. Zander sighed. The Grosvenors were gathering for lunch at their usual venue of a London Italian restaurant to celebrate his mother's birthday. But the plan had been to meet at said restaurant, not at his office.

'Tell them I'll be right down.'

Zander rose and hitched his jacket off the back of his chair, made his way to the marble-floored lobby where his sisters waited. 'Why the escort?'

'To make sure that you actually come.'

'I wouldn't bail on Mum's birthday.'

'Well...just in case. We haven't seen you since

you emailed us that you and Gabby aren't getting married after all.'

'Work has been busy...' It was true enough. He'd thrown himself into work with a ferocious energy, even though he knew he could have delegated many of the tasks he had undertaken himself.

'How are you feeling?'

'I'm fine. It's all worked out for the best.' The words sounded so hollow they echoed.

His sisters exchanged glances.

'Are you sure?' Gemma asked gently.

'Of course I am.'

And if he wasn't fine now he soon would be. Of course he would. At some point surely the palliative effect of work would kick in, relieve these ridiculous symptoms.

The ache he felt in the morning when he woke up, the horrible emptiness of his apartment, the sudden sterility of the furniture he'd once barely noticed. The echoing absence of Gabby, the solitary meals. The obsessive checking of his phone and email in case he'd missed a message. The dreams, and the way his head would turn every time he saw someone who looked even remotely like Gabby.

What was the matter with him?

They approached the restaurant and he halted as he saw Alessio look up towards Gemma, saw the way his best friend's face softened, the sheer love in his eyes.

Suddenly—just like that—he knew exactly what was wrong with him, and came to a sudden halt.

The realisation transfixed him to the spot as knowledge flooded him with its truth. *Dear Lord.* He was an idiot, a fool...denser than platinum. He loved Gabby—*he loved her.* And he had to tell her right now. The urgency was illogical, but absolute. Even if she didn't love him back—and why should she?—he wanted to tell her. He wanted her to know.

Zander turned to his family. 'Sorry, guys. I need to make a call.'

Phone in hand, he raced out. Relief flooded him when she answered the phone.

'Zander?'

'Gabby—where are you?'

'Actually, I'm at Bath Station, about to get on a train to come and see you.'

'You are?'

'Yes.'

'That's brilliant. I'll come and meet you when you get in to London.'

'But—'

'I'll see you in an hour and a half.'

Which didn't give him long.

He raced back inside the restaurant. 'Mum, I love you. Happy birthday! Got to dash. It's an emergency. Not a work one.'

Gabby looked out of the window as the train pulled into the station, wondering anew why Zander had said he'd meet her. Presumably to save her trekking across London to his office? Well, she'd deliver her carefully rehearsed speech and then she could turn around and get on the next train back.

As she alighted from the carriage and headed to the barriers she frowned. That couldn't be Zander, could it? Every iota of her body identified him as the man she loved, but why would he be carrying an enormous bunch of heart-shaped helium balloons?

For a moment hope peeked up over the parapet of pessimism—until suddenly she remembered that it was Laura Grosvenor's birthday.

They must be for his mum. Maybe Frank had asked Zander to pick them up for him, or...

Now she was through the barrier and there was Zander, looking dishevelled, as though he'd raced across London, his face flushed and his hair rumpled.

And so utterly gorgeous.

Her heart ached with love and she yearned to throw her arms around his broad chest. *Bad idea.* She needed to give her rehearsed speech and then leave. At speed. Preferably before he even had a chance to respond.

'Hey,' she said, keeping her eyes away from the balloons, deciding it would be best to ignore them. 'Thank you for coming to meet me. Especially on your mum's birthday. I am *so* sorry. I hope I haven't spoilt the plans?'

'Nope. You haven't. Not at all.' He ran his free hand through his hair. 'Gabby...?'

It was now or never, and she tucked a strand of hair behind her ear and tried to recall her carefully prepared speech. But her brain had become scrambled, messed up by his sheer proximity which seemed to have dispersed every rehearsed word.

The careful explanation, the caveats, the build-up. All gone. Instead, she said, 'I'm here because I love you.'

The words fell from her lips and she closed her eyes, unable to watch his reaction, braced for rejection.

'It's not a big deal. I'm not expecting anything back, and it won't affect how we bring up the baby. I totally get that you don't do love after Claudia.'

She sensed him right in front of her—so close she could inhale his oh-so-familiar citrus smell, so close it took all her willpower not to touch him.

'Open your eyes, Gabby.'

His voice was gentle.

'Look at me. Please?'

The last word disarmed her and she obeyed, looking directly into blue-grey eyes that held a depth of seriousness, warmth and joy.

'I love you, too.' He gave an almost strangled laugh. 'Why do you think I'm standing here with a bunch of balloons?'

Disbelief warred with hope. 'But you can't... I don't understand...'

'I'll try to explain about Claudia. I told you that we had different dreams and ambitions. But it went deeper than that... Very soon into our marriage I realised that I'd made a mistake.'

His breathing was shallow and Gabby stepped closer to him, to offer what comfort she could, sensing he'd never admitted that before.

'We were too different... Perhaps we'd never really known each other. Then she fell ill, and in that awful time the only thing I am glad of is that she never knew. That she believed in our love to the end. And so did everyone else. Because I didn't want to betray her memory, because I felt such guilt.'

'Oh, Zander. I am *so* sorry.' She could see how the guilt, the secrecy, the living a lie would have eaten away at him. Topped up by the guilt at all his success after her death.

'It's OK. I'm telling you because I want you to understand why I believed that love wasn't possible for me. I believed it was *my* fault—that my ambition killed my love and that that would always happen, that it was a given. I'd always put my wishes, my work first. You've made me see that it isn't true. You've made me look back on my marriage differently. Perhaps Claudia and I simply weren't suited and our love simply couldn't have survived our differences because we couldn't ever have worked out a compromise. You've shown me I *can* do that—that *we* can do that. You've shown me that work isn't the be-all and end-all of life, that I can achieve a balance.'

Joy lightened her whole body and she felt as if she must be radiating happiness.

'And you've changed *me*. Brought me out of my comfort zone, encouraged me to try new things and overcome my fears and anxiety.' Gabby grinned. 'You've shown me how to have fun, take some risks, to sing and be heard and seen. Before I set out today I even sent my book off to some agents. I spent so much of my child-hood, my life, feeling afraid, thinking I had to be invisible or quiet or perfect. You've helped me figure out who I am. The real me. Made me see I *am* good enough, and that some things are worth risking rejection for.'

'I'm thrilled about your book. And this is what I hope we'll do for the rest of our lives. Grow to-gether, learn together, discover new things. *To-gether.* I want to make a home with you. Ever since you entered my house I've realised how bland it is, how dull… I want a *real* home, full of love and clutter and…you.'

Gabby grinned at him. It seemed impossible

to smile as widely as her happiness dictated. 'I'd love to take you shopping, to all the markets and places I love. We can choose colours together, paint walls, make the happiest home in the world.'

'I love you, Gabby. I love everything you've achieved. I love your courage, your loyalty and your love for your grandparents. I love the way you overcame your fears. I admire your resilience. I love the way you tuck your hair behind your ears. I love *you*.'

'I love you, too—your strength, the way you've coped with dyslexia, your drive and ambition, your love for your family, the amount you care... I just *love* you, Zander. This baby is the luckiest baby in the world to have a dad like you.'

'And a mum like you. So...now seems the right moment for this.'

Turning, he made a slight movement with his hands and suddenly from the crowds emerged a group of people holding instruments. Before Gabby even knew what was happening a jazz melody broke out, the strains upbeat and beautiful, and a woman began to sing, her voice rich and melodious.

And then Zander released the balloons and

went down on one knee, pulling a box from his

'Gabby. Will you marry me and make me the
happiest man in the stratosphere?'

And this time he slid the ring on to her finger
and looked up with a smile. 'Diamonds, lapis
lazuli and sapphires. Love and friendship for a
lifetime. We are going to be the happiest family
in the whole entire universe.'

And as he picked her up, twirled her around
and then pulled her into a deep, soul-satisfying,
toe-curling kiss, Gabby knew that they would be.

LET'S TALK
Romance

For exclusive extracts, competitions and special offers, find us online:

- facebook.com/millsandboon
- @millsandboonuk
- @millsandboon

Or get in touch on 0844 844 1351*

For all the latest titles coming soon, visit millsandboon.co.uk/nextmonth

*Calls cost 7p per minute plus your phone company's price per minute access charge

Want even more
ROMANCE?

Join our bookclub today!